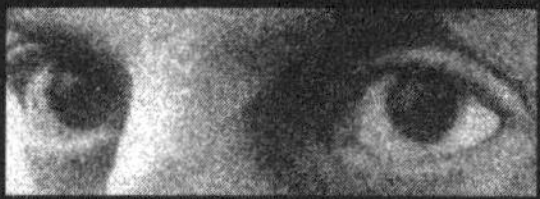

The Passive Vampire

Ghérasim Luca

THE PASSIVE VAMPIRE

WITH AN INTRODUCTION ON THE
OBJECTIVELY OFFERED OBJECT

a found portrait
and
seventeen illustrations

Translated and introduced by Krzysztof Fijałkowski

TWISTED SPOON PRESS
PRAGUE

ISBN 978-80-86264-31-8

CONTENTS

ILLUSTRATIONS

LUCA THE ABSOLUTE

If the name Ghérasim Luca remains known only to a few (and almost to no one outside France and Romania) then it is tempting to believe that this is no more than his wish. Born of a disappearance – at the time of his first publication the writer chose his new name from an obituary notice – dedicating much of his work to conjuring the void at the heart of language and of existence itself, and consigned to a wilful absence in his chosen death, Luca's presence quickens like a magic cipher that appears and fades again before anyone can reread its handwriting.

On February 9, 1994, Luca wrote to his companion to tell her that he was going to throw himself into the Seine. An extraordinary text written in 1945, *La Mort morte* (Dead Death), had already announced the fragile dialectic between life and its negation: an account of five suicide attempts, each accompanied by a farewell note and an automatic text written during the act. Yet somehow death is the last thing one thinks of when reading through the small pile of incandescent books he left behind. That so much of Luca's writing invokes silence, disappearance, and absence would seem to suggest that he was searching for the very means to cheat despair, for ways to reinvent love, language, the world and a poet's place in it.

More than a decade later, Luca's work seems increasingly precious, not only as a missing piece of the history of international surrealism – that of the Bucharest surrealist group (1940-47) – and as a hidden precursor for several elements of contemporary thought (notably Deleuze and Guattari's *Anti-Oedipus*, prefigured over a quarter of a century earlier by Luca's "non-Oedipal" theories), but also as a fixed marker for the questions asked today by those wishing to situate themselves in the continuing stream of a critical surrealist thought and against those demoralising currents with which the new century, too, is awash. Luca and Trost's *Dialectics of the Dialectic* (1945) addressed this question in a tone that confronted desperation with defiance:

> The inexhaustible diversity of the means of cretinisation at the disposal of the enemies of the dialectical development of thought and of action, and the oceans of blood which bear witness to the current cessation of objective evolution, will never make us avert our eyes, even for a moment, from the red thread of Reality.

Dialectics of the Dialectic was the capital text (albeit a divisive one) for the Romanian Surrealist Group, whose core comprised the writers Ghérasim Luca, Gellu Naum, Paul Paun, Virgil Teodorescu, and Dolfi Trost, and with links to the painters Victor Brauner, Jacques Hérold, and Jules Pérahim. Formed in the wake of the outbreak of hostilities in 1939 but unable to publish or exhibit during the war years, which had already been preceded by a period of increasing censorship in Romania, the group nevertheless led an active covert existence, the direction it took both extending and giving a radical slant to the primarily French surrealism of the 1930s. As such, their activities suggested, for example, the confrontation between the poetic rigour of André Breton and the hysterical extremism of Salvador Dalí at a time when the Paris group itself had abandoned attempts to resolve these divergences. A distress call from a band of poets marooned in Eastern Europe, *Dialectics of the Dialectic* affirmed unshakeable fidelity to Breton, dialectical materialism, and objective chance while also having the temerity to warn the international movement of the dangers of becoming just another artistic style. It proposed instead a reinvention of the surrealist imagination: a critical approach to dreams, the eroticisation of the proletariat, the poetic appropriation of quantum physics, and the perpetual re-evaluation of surrealism through the negation of negation.

One senses that Luca was a key figure in these developments, and his own contributions to the group's direction were amongst the most interesting. As a teenager he had already been a member of the confrontational Alge group (1930-33), and with the Bucharest avant-garde increasingly fascinated with surrealist ideas, by late 1938 Luca and Naum were both in Paris and had established contact with the French surrealists. On the declaration of war, they were obliged to return to Bucharest, but were now committed to continuing surrealist activity, even in clandestine form.

Luca's writing of this period, often in French, alternates polemic with delirious narrative. *The Inventor of Love* from 1945 is an exposition of non-oedipal theory, advocating the paroxysm of love and sexuality as the means to overcome Oedipal oppression. The shorter text *I Love You* (1942) reads like a detective's fingertip search of a bedroom, a single sentence capped with a question mark in which objects gradually impose themselves as the mirrors and the sorcerers of a lover lost amid the dust. Projects such as his "cubomania" collages, on the other hand, propose a graphic equivalent to this reinvention of the world by cutting an image into squares and reassembling them, as if once again the simplest theoretical techniques should be taken to their extreme conclusions.

Luca left Bucharest for Paris in 1952. While maintaining close contacts with associates of the Parisian surrealist group such as fellow Romanian Brauner and Sarane Alexandrian, he nevertheless chose to follow a more solitary, secretive path. His writing, now more clearly poetry rather than prose, became more spare and hermetic, following Raymond Roussel and Michel Leiris in pursuit of the hidden tracks of the French tongue through verbal games, stammerings, and the dismantling of words, as though to dissolve and recast the very elements of language and meaning:

> elle est bien morte la mort
> la mort folle la morphologie de la
> la morphologie de la métamorphose de l'orgie
>
> (*La Contre-créature*, 1953)

Such untranslatable poems enlist a "verbal alchemy" to conjure up and celebrate the presence/absence of the loved one (*Aimée à jamais*), to confront the threat of nuclear catastrophe (*La Clef*), to question how to live in the face of the world's despair ("How to get out without leaving?" he asked), or to dialecticise the void of death (*Autres secrets du vide et du plein*). Compelling performances and recordings were made of some of these works; Gilles

Deleuze announced Luca as "the greatest French poet." With an intensity and seriousness that suggest that such poetry will eventually replace what today we call philosophy, Luca's words commanded the silencing of silence:

> If it is true, as is claimed
> that after death man continues
> a phantom existence
> I'll let you know
>
> (*La Mort morte*, 1945)

The present volume, though it represents a mere fraction of Luca's earlier work, is considered central to his thought, not only as the culmination of his journey into surrealism throughout the 1930s, but as a substantially more elaborate and extended text than most of the writings by the Bucharest group of that period. Published in 1945 by the fictitious (and significantly named) Éditions de l'Oubli, supposedly in Paris – in fact, of course, in Bucharest – *Le Vampire passif* announced a print run of only 460 copies plus another 41 in a deluxe format. Though examples seem to have circulated with reasonable liberty in France during the following decade, its rarity until its reissue by José Corti in 2001 had made it something of a lost legend within surrealist literature, rarely referred to and almost never seen other than in jealously guarded private libraries.

But despite its status as a singular, in places even delirious text, there is much in the tone and ideas of *The Passive Vampire* to situate it firmly within the traditions and canon of surrealist writing. Stylistic homages and direct references to Sade, Huysmans, or to clinical textbooks, for example, are consistent with the interests of French surrealist authors. And as the book progresses, its deranged logic, its lurching from a frantic cataloguing and collaging of irrational ingredients to a dispassionate, even scientific precision, and eventually to the transparent borrowings from unacknowledged sources, point to Lautréamont's *Chants de Maldoror* – perhaps the single most cherished text among the first generation of surrealists – as its black genie. Indeed, the appeal to the archetypal figure of the vampire probably owes more to the manic Gothic of *Maldoror* than to the currency of popular legends from Luca's part of Europe.

At the same time, however, *The Passive Vampire* is also a meditation on the writings of the French surrealists themselves, and in particular André Breton's, whose books such as *Mad Love, Communicating Vessels,* and *Nadja* (specifically referenced in these pages) stand as ghost readers for Luca's text. Its grave tone, its adoption of a first-person confessional that insists on narrative as fact, however much credulity is strained (I personally remain convinced that everything in this book did indeed happen),[1] its meticulous accounts and dissections of the smallest events, supported with photographic evidence, and the pursuit of a love that might also be a form of haunting, all recall Breton's signature style, and it is to the absent poet that much of the book seems dedicated.

Of course, the recurring themes of an encounter between psychoanalysis, psychosis, and the object – explored in the form of a game of "Objectively Offered Objects," which serves as a disorienting prologue to "The Passive Vampire" and then infects that text with its secret exchanges – would all appear familiar to readers of the French surrealist group's journal of the early 1930s, *Le Surréalisme au service de la Révolution.* In its pages Salvador Dalí first masterminded the game of "Symbolically Functioning Objects": fragile constructions of often everyday found items put together apparently at random by the game's participants and then subjected to analysis. The objects of *The Passive Vampire,* photographed by Théodore Brauner (brother of Victor), seem to have been lost or abandoned on Luca's emigration from Romania, but both their documentation and their scrupulous interpretation clearly situate them within the category of the surrealist object that played such a prominent role in surrealism from the 1930s onwards.[2]

Just as Paris is a principal character of so many French surrealist texts, Bucharest is curiously present in *The Passive Vampire*. But the Bucharest of late 1941, when the book was first written, has a very different status for its author. Most obviously, it is a city under effective occupation, controlled by the pro-Nazi Iron Guard whose rise to power in autumn 1940 (the period when at least some of the action described in Luca's narrative took place, in particular a major earthquake) signalled a definitive end to the distinctive avant-garde activity of the already repressive 1930s. Luca's membership of that avant-garde (his writings had even earned him a brief spell in prison) and above all his status as a Jew, would have made his position doubly precarious in a city that herein feels poised on the brink of disaster. Luca, like all surrealists, hated any idea of national identity, but clearly he detested Bucharest and its inhabitants as well. Forced by the conflict to leave France, an expulsion he experienced as a kind of trauma, his heart nonetheless remained there; in February 1940 he wrote to Jacques Hérold that "not for a moment can I for-get that I am no longer in Paris. It is my one obsession, and it sits well with my persecution mania."[3]

That Luca should be writing to a Romanian friend in French, as seems to have been standard practice among Romanian surrealist émigrés, is also significant. While French acted as *lingua franca* among intellectuals across much of Central and Eastern Europe in the nineteenth and early twentieth centuries, the adoption of it by the Bucharest surrealists of the 1940s signals not only a deliberate abandoning of the "native" tongue, but that their intended audience remained above all the French surrealist group (even if the latter's dispersal on the four winds meant they would be in no position to hear these messages, let alone reply).

If in 1941 Luca is already writing letters to friends in French, it seems reasonable that his published texts, too, would be composed directly in the language rather than translated, and this poses several issues for the translator of *Le Vampire passif.* On the one hand, certain phrases feel a little stiff, their tone at times perhaps still stretching for the rhythm of the library of French books Luca must have had at his bedside (literally or figuratively, since he hints here at having to leave it behind in France) with a formality befitting the challenging stare one sees repeatedly in photographs of him. On the other, Luca's constructions tend to remain simple, unambiguous at the level of grammar even when their implications are puzzling, or when they are piled pell-mell one on another. Words seem to be chosen and placed quite deliberately, sometimes in unusually long sentences, with a vocabulary of concrete expressions that includes, for instance, a number of unfamiliar medical or cabalistic terms: the poetry of Lautréamont's *Poésies,* not the allusive lyrical imagery of Paul Éluard, even when the book slides from description to mania and then into a frenzy of language. I have therefore chosen wherever possible to opt for the most direct, literal translations, respecting con-structions and syntax, thinking that any shifts in form over the course of the book should be seen as both integral to the original and perfectly deliberate on the author's part.[4]

This translation has been a long time coming, a process started perhaps on the day in November 1988 when I first met Ghérasim Luca himself to talk about the events of this book that now seemed powerfully remote from its author and was to become something of an obsession for me. I could not, however, have brought it to fruition without the precious contributions of several people. Firstly, the help and advice of Guy Flandre, whose devoted knowledge of both Luca and his work, as well as corrections of early drafts of the translation, have been invaluable.

Our grateful thanks, too, go to Fabienne Raphoz and Bertrand Fillaudeau at José Corti for their support and advice. Finally, though, the two individuals closest to Ghérasim Luca have lent this work their blessing, their guidance, and their singular experience: Micheline Catti in Paris and Antonia Rasicovici in Saint Louis, and it is to them that this translation is dedicated.

KRZYSZTOF FIJAŁKOWSKI
2008

The Objectively Offered Object

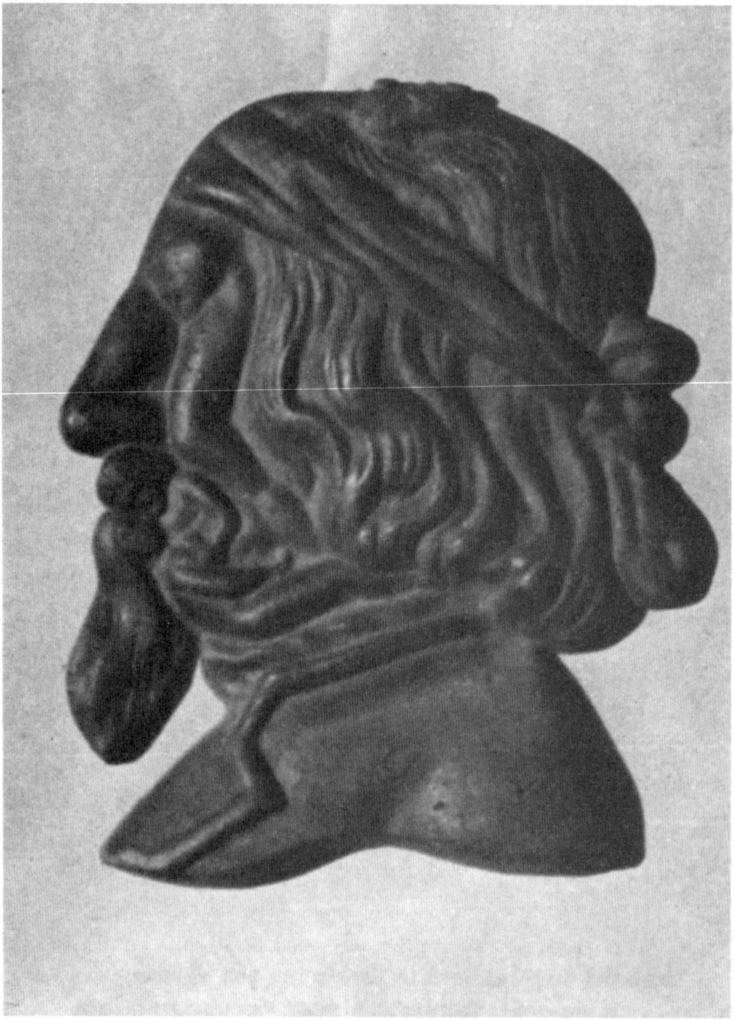

Ghérasim Luca revealed by objective chance (found portrait)

My few experiences of an obsessional and delirious contact with certain objects – the determination of chance having inexorably led to their encounter or construction – have given me the opportunity to discover a new object of knowledge to add to the ranks of known objects (dream objects, symbolically functioning objects, real and virtual, mobile and mute, phantom and ready-made objects),[1] a new objective possibility for resolving dialectically the conflict between interior and exterior worlds, an experiment the surrealist movement has made its raison d'être since the First Manifesto. A game with a pronounced megalomaniac character was the origin of my encounter with a new object projected by desire, one that threw a fascinating and terrible light on the internal life of humankind. The game, during which my friends and I discovered a symbolic form of expression with which to oppose a general persecution mania, consisted of a reciprocal bestowal of decorations, allowing us the simultaneous pleasure of giving and of receiving, a pleasure which the inmate of the Central Psychiatric Hospital who had given us the idea for the game had achieved by the partial means of self-decoration. In creating these decorations, the first objectively offered object (O.O.O.) was produced. Naturally, the act of bestowing decorations and the limited psychic drives relating to it are of little importance compared to the limitless psychic motivations connected with the far-reaching act of giving. Using the decoration as a fixed point of departure, the offered object is able to blossom in all its dynamic and multiple complexity.

For a found or made object to be transformed into an offered object, and for it to be able to change its nature in line with the new relationships established in the interior life of the individual seeking a new balance between the internal and external, the pretext to this transformation must have an interpretative value that is, if not always negligible, at least very limited. The offering of an object might have as its setting the pretext of a decoration, or a celebration, or some other external and circumstantial accident, just as the manifest life of a dream uses diurnal remnants and random internal and external stimuli to provide the sleeper a framework of no interpretational value within which the action of the dream can unfold. All that is left as the essential and determining element in the dream, as in the act of offering an object, is desire seeking fulfillment within this setting-pretext with a view to its hastening transformation into the desire's reality.

But this is not the only technical resemblance between the elaboration of a dream and the offered object. The creation of objects and their bestowal upon someone who has been rigorously selected through the symbolic nature of these objects establish between individuals relationships founded on an active collective unconscious, which until now only dreams have set in a workable mechanism common to us all. In turn poetry, which at a certain moment Lautréamont proposed in anticipation of this supremely lyrical phase,* brings the automatic structures of this mechanism within our grasp. The offered object allows the introduction of this active collective unconscious into conscious and direct relationships between individuals, relations that even an elementary interpretation would illuminate to be as subversive, strange, and revealing as those of dreams.

In today's society, the offered object bears no qualitative relation to the gift. The gift is an object that is bestowed only after having been stripped of its objective

* "Poetry should be made by all. Not by one."[2]

erotic character. Its emotive force is neutralised by its standardisation, which has allowed the bourgeoisie to thwart the differentiation of individual tendencies and thus offer one more argument in support of contemporary morality, which is presented as the only all-encompassing morality possible.* Flowers and chocolates have virtually become the calling cards of disinterested love and the paying of one's respects. The gift of a flower, which might be treated as a very powerful object of aphrodisiac knowledge, becomes within the confused and banal mechanism to which present society assigns it a neutralised, commonplace object in the world of external things. The analysis of the gift of a flower is impossible in most cases, since this choice comes from habit and a resigned submission to reality. Because offered objects deny this reality-obstacle, and oppose it in a conflict that favours desire, they are subject to the damaging discipline of censorship. The offered object retains the bizarre appearance of the dream image but, like dream images, it will not hide its latent and determining content from interpretative analysis.

A greater number of fortuitous encounters can be

* Bourgeois love, practised within defined forms, runs from the useless engagement present to the useful and costly wedding gift via the two quantitative phases of the same sentimentalism.

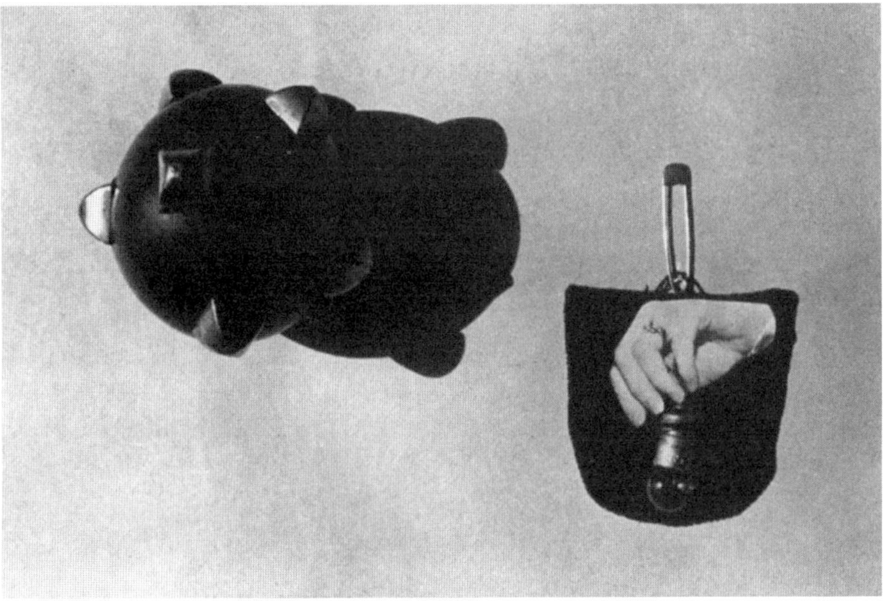

Fig. 1 Diurnal and Nocturnal Displacement

brought about by the law of objective chance since the offered object harnesses chance in a dynamic and dramatic form through its lyrical and emotional appearance, through its objective value of interpretation leading directly to knowledge, and above all, through the total transformation it imposes upon relationships between individuals – a transformation that becomes the somnambulistic manifestation of the collective unconscious in its waking state, thus consummating its nocturnal dream form.[3] The found object, in other words, the object we offer to ourselves, only succeeds in exercising a small proportion of the possibilities for the bewildering appearance of chance. When offering an object to someone, external causality responds more rapidly to internal necessities. Erotic relations between myself and other individuals are more quickly established through the mediation of the object. The object that is found but not offered is an object of knowledge, albeit through masturbation. The search for a found object destined to be offered multiplies external causality and stamps objective chance with the rhythm of internal necessity. Sometimes hostile, sometimes favourable in its attitudes, the ambivalence of our libidinous disposition forces chance to correspond to this disposition, and helps its appearance through the giving of objects. We force chance's appearance and objectivisation, since our tendencies to love/hate find an almost continuous equivalence in the world of external objects. In general, I would refuse any object that wished to castrate me, but would be glad to find and offer such an object to someone for whom I had an especially aggressive erotic attraction or repulsion. In the complexity of collective erotic relationships, the satisfaction of desire is facilitated by this permanent exchange of sperm in the form of the offered object. In moving from the found and self-offered object to the offered object, from masturbation to priapism, objective chance has made such a leap that its typical rarity (to which the notion of chance has almost always been linked) disappears completely, its heightened worth having become endlessly accessible to our dialectically permanent and sadistic activity.

V.: a starfish attached to a spoon.[4]

To attach the spoon to the starfish I used an axe, a nail, and a long thread. This all-too directly pederastic operation lasted almost an hour, during which time I became extremely annoyed. If the action had taken place in a dream, it would certainly have been a nightmare. The spoon, which being male represents me, recalls a phrase from one of my books: "the soup spoon, another depth of the ocean," which suggests to me that it is I who is considering taking V.'s place, the bisexuality of erotic tendencies, and the active-passive homosexual position.

Hélène: a ball with nails hammered into it (fig. 1).[5]

To begin with, this attempted to express a homage, or rather a response to a homage. She liked the balls I had in my room, and she had expressed the desire to have one. This desire to possess one of the balls, which from the moment I found them I interpreted as symbolising testicles, enchanted me. I gave myself the pleasure of offering her a ball, and could not understand why I had not done this straightaway. I did not give it to her immediately because the offering of a testicle in front of others would have been embarrassing. A week later, this embarrassment over a public offering was more easily bearable thanks to the presence of a pretext to the bestowal of decorations.

As well as the necessity of offering her the ball, but in a manner that was not exhibitionistic, there was the external causality of Hélène's absence, giving chance a double objectivity. My desire was fulfilled just as in a dream, in other words, by retaining one of its customary deformations: displacement. Instead of the disappearance of everyone else, which would have allowed me to offer the ball to

Hélène, it was Hélène who vanished, something that did nothing to change the essential relationship between myself, her, and the ball. Through the intervention of chance, the offer of the ball was executed in the conditions I had desired a week before.

When H. had expressed her desire to own a ball, my reaction should have been the reverse of what was dictated by reality. But the impulse towards pleasure only retained the element favourable to it within reality, the ball. Figure 1 (a single ball) was forgotten as a negligible detail precisely because it was the most important and painful one. H. had expressed her desire to possess a ball, which was the equivalent of the desire to castrate me, to deny me as a male, equivalent to a refusal. She was repelled by the exhibitionistic display of my testicles. If I had taken account of the number 1, I would surely never have offered H. the ball. But I offered it anyway, since (opposing reality and favouring pleasure) the ball had become a love object. "Love object" was the text I attached to the ball, and on the pin with which I attached it I wrote "Hélène shuddered" in order to guarantee to myself in advance that this love object would move her. Thanks to this choice of text, made several days after H.'s request, it would seem that the mutilating nature of this request was beginning to reveal itself. In order to reject this unpleasurable motivation, I wrote "Hélène shuddered" on the object just as I would in a dream, as an action accomplished, as a desire that was fulfilled because, in reality, H. was not shuddering at all.

The object received from H. in reply (fig. 1: a partially clenched hand grasping the end of a light bulb, both of these placed on a piece of velvet) confirmed the sadistic-mutilatory intentions of refusal and repulsion. The hand, having wrenched off the testicle, drops it onto a piece of velvet, with the velvet becoming the castrating dish of Salomé and the castrating veil of Veronica.

P.: two objects resembling a pair of earrings.[6]

The object had been intended for P.'s wife. For reasons of an aesthetic nature I refused to offer objects resembling earrings to a woman since, thanks to their new owner, they would become too commonplace as objects. In refusing to give them to a woman, I also denied myself the satisfaction of giving payment to a woman, or rather of frequenting a brothel I had heard about in which the women cost several thousand francs. I refused to give the earrings to a woman because in theory the idea of paying her humiliates me, an idea that conflicts with the idea of paying her just the same. In rejecting the idea of paying a woman, I stifle the desire to pay her, provoking the following aesthetic argument: since it is all too common to offer earrings to a woman, I will therefore offer them to a man to differentiate myself.

In this conflict, which seems to culminate in the triumph of reality (aesthetic reason), desire finds its favourable outcome in the other aspect of my bisexuality. I offer the earrings to a man, taking advantage of the rule of aesthetic motivation that masks the subversiveness of my immoral impulse. The aesthetic reason I invoke is a representation of reality, but at the same time desire uses it against the reality from which it comes.

G.: a glass tube, the number 7, and a flat spool.[7]

The choice of a glass tube stems from the manifest, almost conscious sympathy I felt for G. on the day I made the decorations. I delayed giving him the object for as long as possible, knowing that he would enjoy it and would discern its erotic form. The latter was only vaguely erotic, since the glass tube was very thin, but I was certain he would notice it and would be happy to be given, in the form of a decoration, a male member.

The choice of the longest possible object made of such fragile material was not accidental. The first object I had seen in the shop's display window was the head of a siphon, which I wanted to take only once I had purchased the other things. Although I had seen the siphon several times while searching among the objects on display, I left having forgotten to ask the shopkeeper for it. I did not keep the siphon because its obvious pederastic significance could not slip past my censoring mechanisms unnoticed. The head of the siphon could only be accepted in its new form as a thin glass tube.

If I did not take the siphon, it was also because I refused to give a man a male member that could then be used to attract all women to him. So instead I offered G. an object whose male sexual form he could grasp, but one that would also threaten him: if he takes my women, his member will break. My bisexual tendencies are permanently indissoluble because the threat of breaking the male member is a deflowering rather than a castration. The pederastic character of this threat appeared all the more forcefully given that C.N.,[8] whom I know mainly through G., had suffered mental breakdowns characterised by a constant fear of breaking the bottom of his glass.

The number 7 was chosen mindlessly. Though not as compromised as the number 13, both occupy a similar level of banal mystery. I was looking for a number on a plate covered in dust and tokens. When I looked at my fingers, I noticed that they were dirty, something that annoyed me for no particular reason given that I was not concerned about my cleanliness. I was aware of the need for cleanliness, having had it drummed into me, just as I'd been taught that 7 is a mystery number. I chose the number 7 because of the mindless state that was provoked by a sudden feeling of mind-destroying hygiene, and with it, the number 22. I preferred to place a 7 on G.'s decoration because 22 made me think of Aurèle Z, Aurèle C. and Aurèle B in the poem *R101,* in which all three die at that age and in which even the poem's title contains the repetition of a number which again makes 2. The association between the number 22 and A.B.'s poem, in which the poets die at the age of 22, stems from the macabre association ascribed to the number 13, and thus also to the number 7.[9]

I attached the number 7, which would kill G., to the decoration in a way that was altered by the process of elaborating it (the glass tube), because the number 22, which would kill him too directly, would not have passed censorship (the siphon).

As for the flat spool, I was aware of my disappointment at losing it, and could see no reason at all to give it away since I had not even been asked to do so. When I am asked

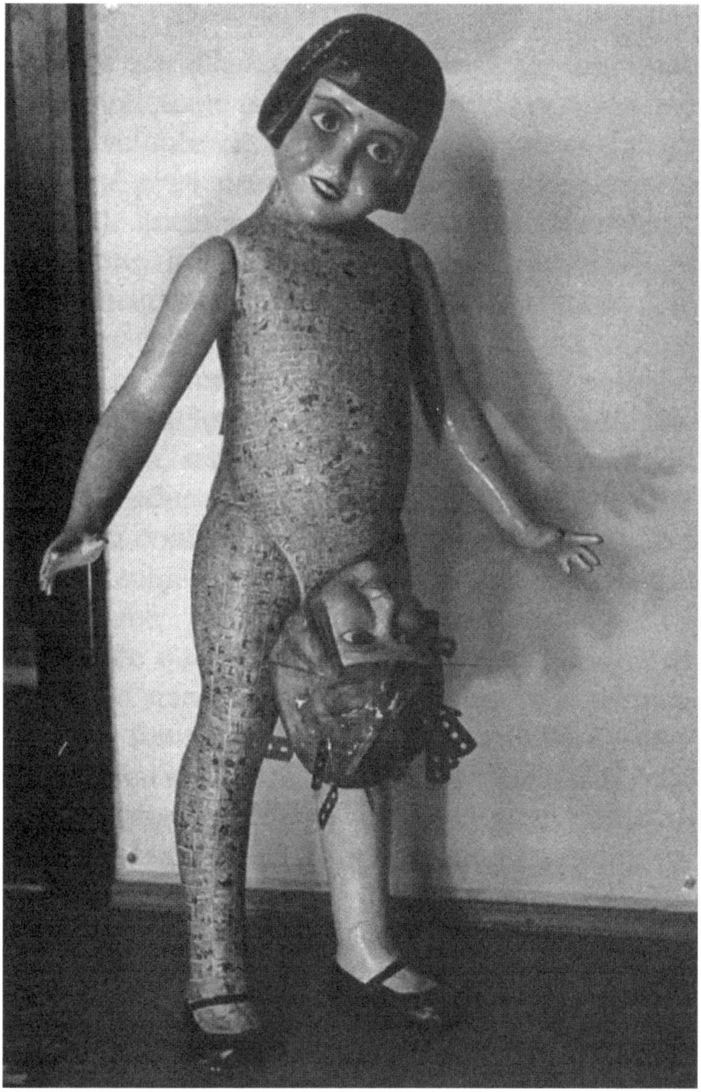

Fig. 2 The Letter L

for objects I have collected, I generally refuse to give them because a relationship between myself and the object is always established, one that is too well known to need explanation. I had found the spool in a street in Paris, where it had no doubt been thrown away. Its design resembled a highly ornate mediaeval coat of arms, and the petty commercial utility it had adopted gave it a humorous aspect that I subsequently continued to enjoy. I brought the object home and placed it among the others on my bookshelf.

Suddenly, without any discernable motive, and even though the conscious impulse opposing the gesture was fairly strong, I took the spool out of the drawer and added it to G.'s decoration. This was put first on G.'s chest, then placed among his other objects on the shelf of his own library. The desire to have the books I had left behind in Paris was stronger than the desire to keep the spool. So long as the spool was in my home, in a drawer, I was separated from my books. I put the spool on G.'s bookshelf, just as I had placed it on my own in Paris, and I got the books back. On it I wrote "Where must I leave you?", the question I had asked of it since I could not decide whether to leave it on the nocturnal bookshelf in Paris or G.'s real bookshelf. I was tempted to leave it on my Paris bookshelf, so I interrogated it so as to know where to put it, and now it was I who was the chauffeur, driving my customer, the spool, back again. The spool came by car from the station to my bookshelf, and the car bore the number 7.

I chose the macabre number 7 because I envied G. for having brought all of his books back with him.

André Breton: *The Letter L* (fig. 2).

While browsing in some antique shops, I noticed a doll in one window looking at me, but I did not stop. A few weeks later, I awoke earlier than usual one morning and went straight to the antique shop to buy the doll I had refused to meet. Not knowing the reason why, I had cut several hundred riddles from the pages of some Hachette almanacs and put them into a number of envelopes. Returning home, I produced the envelopes and pasted the riddles at random onto the torso and one leg of the doll. Next I attached another doll's head upside-down against its groin. Despite the monotony of the work, I continued applying the riddles, even while receiving a visitor, such was my state of permanent excitement in making this object. I decided to cover this second doll's head with a mask made of steel pen nibs. Since I did not know how to sew, I asked my wife to make the mask. She made a start, but rapidly tired of the task and began to make excuses, becoming ill-tempered and irritating me in turn. I hid the object out of sight, since its unpleasant appearance was only increasing my irritation. We argued, and the next day I moved out to stay with friends. After a week I returned to continue making the object I thought I had abandoned for good. I found that razor blades inserted into the doll's head would be a good substitute for the mask of pen nibs. One of the razor blades sliced the doll's eye in two. My wife was delighted that the incident had come to a close and that I had resumed the process of making the object, the interruption of which had been her doing. She had come back from staying with a friend, the mother of a little girl just a few months old.* Pointing at the doll, she asked me what we were going to call our child. I didn't appreciate the mediocrity of this association, and replied harshly that the object couldn't be our child since it would be called Nadja. The object was finished the next day, and was titled *The Letter L.*

So long as the relationship between myself and the doll was that of a seeking subject to an object asking to be found, the doll remained neutral and indifferent. I did not wish to find the doll; what I wanted was the bronze letter R I had brought home with me (fig. 4) and a hairdresser's waxen dummy head (fig. 5). From the moment the object

* The little girl died two months after I made the object.

broke free of me, using me as a spectator-actor mediating between myself and Breton, the undesirable object was transformed and took on a character of its own. Now qualitatively different, it exercised extraordinary pressure on me. I took the doll away with me, even though I had yet to seek it out. Indifferent and mute as long as it was asking to be found, the object, which had now been found so that it could be offered, began to murmur a black-magical language between myself and Breton, one that was very close to dream and to primordial language. This secret and mysterious communication lasted uninterrupted for several days. Every riddle glued to the woman's body, having been chosen at random from the envelope, gave me the satisfaction I would have gained from a conversation (?) with Breton in Paris. I had refused the invitations from several friends who wanted to introduce me to him and, apart from a brief conversation at the Gradiva Gallery in 1938, my contact with B. was limited to an exchange of letters and our mutual friendship with Victor Brauner. The dreadful, intimidating inhibition he inspired in me ultimately got the better of my great desire to know him.

The doll found in the shopwindow and the envelope full of riddles in the drawer only imposed their presence, violently, into my life at the moment when the desire to know

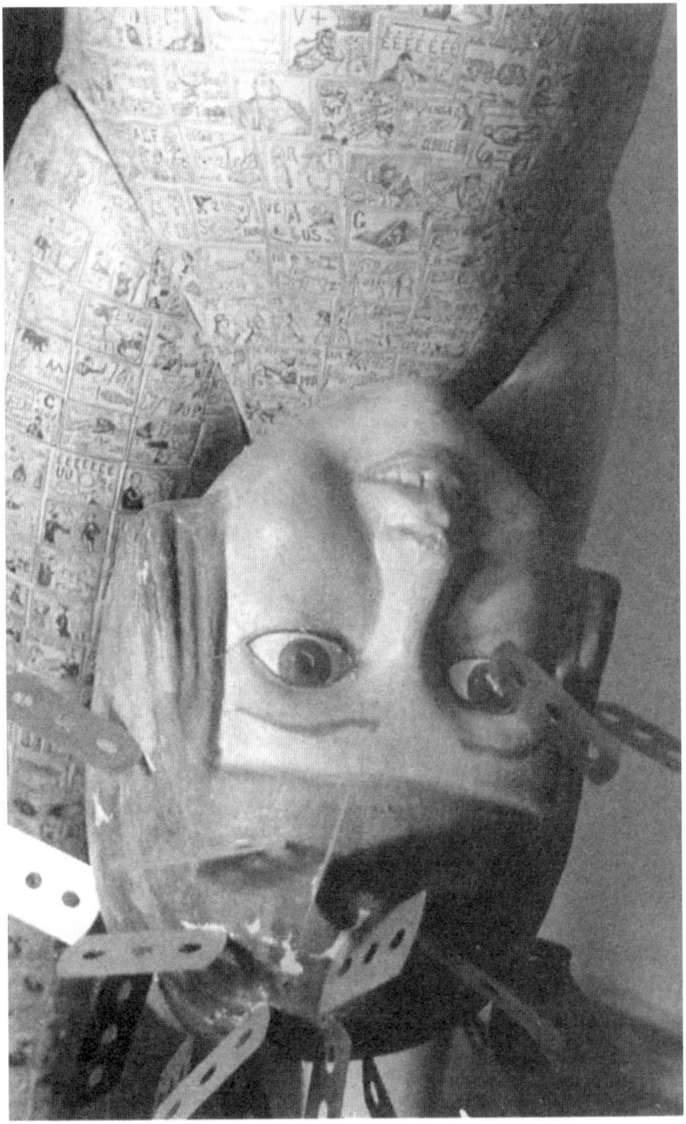

Fig. 3 The Letter L (detail)

B. located in them the overt substitute means for doing this. The incubus found its full realisation through the use of these two magic objects in which I was also shortly to discern sorcery's demonic power.

I had intended to cover the head over the doll's groin with a mask of steel pen nibs. The idea for this mask probably hid a final censoring attempt to keep control over the strictly intellectual sphere within which desire struggled. But my wife refused to construct the mask because, in identifying herself with me, she refused to put the relationship between myself and B. on an intellectual level. The head replacing the sex had to remain free and erect. When I immediately hid the doll, thus breaking off all contact with B., the incubus could not continue because a nightmare brought on by this undistorted admission of desire forcefully awakened me. I also interrupted the construction of the object because my wife,* in identifying herself with me, intended to change the incubus into a succubus, something I rejected with a double jealousy.

We didn't speak to each other for a week, and I moved out to stay with friends. My sudden return home to continue making the object was the result of discovering that I could

* Like my wife, the two heads both had their hair in what is known here as a "Breton" hairstyle.

satisfy my desire towards B. while avoiding painful consequences and at the same time have the means to take revenge on the double infidelity committed by my wife and B. I mutilated the head (the sex) using several razor blades and, as a supreme ejaculation, with the last one I sliced the doll's eye. This convulsive-sadistic action thus took on a concrete, bewitching value.

Once again I resisted my wife's thinly-veiled attempts to insinuate herself into my relationship with B. when, pointing at the doll, she asked me what name we should give to our child (this time, however, she no longer harboured any intention of having me replaced, remaining content with a *ménage à trois*). But my reply was such as to antagonise us both. "Nadja" was a title that distanced my wife completely from my relationship with B., but I was separated from him as well since I could only ever be a spectator between Nadja and Breton. I was in a foul mood until the following morning, when I decided to change the offered object's name.

The Letter L not only evoked a passage from *Nadja,** but also a pretext-passage in the preface of my book *The Anatomy of the Letter*[11] in which I was no longer just a spectator/traveler, but a creator/exhibitionist instead, and this

* "But what, according to Nadja, constitutes the chief interest of the page, without my managing to learn why, is the calligraphy of the L's."[10]

fact succeeded in removing Nadja entirely from the relationship between herself and Breton that I had inadvisably re-established the previous day without their knowing it.

Victor Brauner: *Dusk* (fig. 6).

The pen nibs, which had a censorial function in covering and rationalising the genitals on the object offered to Breton, here took on their direct symbolism now that they sat on a velvet cushion. The 75 exposed penises on a red cushion produced such pain in the back and kidneys, dizziness, and partial blindness in the woman sewing them on that she had to interrupt her work and lie down. She had just learned that a doctor's wife had been raped by thirty men during a pogrom and was taken to hospital with a severe haemorrhage. I did not count the pen nibs at the point she stopped working to lie down, but I am certain she stopped symptomatically at the thirtieth. The next day she began the work again without difficulties and sewed on all the remaining nibs. The first problem arose when I asked her to fix a celluloid hand among the nibs. She vigorously refused the masturbation of the 75 erect penises as it would have made her miss out on such an extraordinary orgy.

The symptomatology of this refusal was likewise translated into her total inability to secure the hand onto the cushion, which she only overcame after my entreaties, but even then only in such a way as to leave the fingers as far as possible from the nibs, several centimetres above the cushion. I showed her where I wanted the thread to go and, to her great surprise, the hand readily moved to the place I had envisaged for it.

My intention was to have 75 nibs sewn onto the cushion so as to form the outline of a head, but I abandoned this plan as there would have been nowhere to place the hand. I abandoned the representation of a head since I wanted at all costs to sew on the hand.

I noticed among my objects two pen nibs representing a head and a hand, both received from Victor Brauner two years before (fig. 7). I immediately perceived the general erotic significance of the object I offered V.B., which was a reply to the provocation issued by the two nibs he had given me. The attempt at seduction and the symbolic proposal of mutual masturbation were accepted (and perhaps desired) by me, and the regressive erotic content was revealed by the exchange of two objects masturbating one another.

The latent material of desire, symptomatically realised by the exchange of the two objects, could also be verified by the parallel analysis of our diurnal and nocturnal practices.

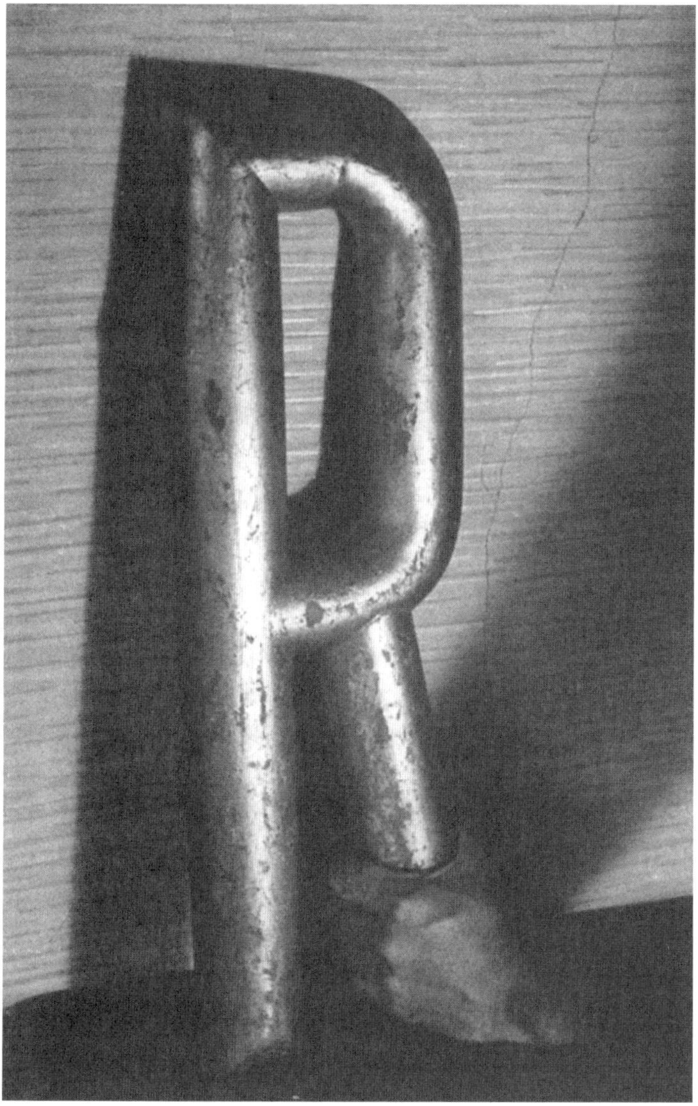

Fig. 4 Revolution First

V.B.'s diurnal masturbatory practice of collecting pencil sharpeners, which I had followed from the start with the greatest interest, corresponded to the general masturbatory aspect presented to me through dreams before and after the analysis, driven by the castration complex. These erotic, plastic, and nocturnal practices confirmed this isolated practice.

Between the legs hanging below the cushion, the two distinct elements upon the cushion – the hand and the penis – came together so as to become inseparable. The ideal masturbation realised by this hand/penis dispelled any doubt that might have existed over the object's significance.

Before becoming a hand/penis, the hand bore two numbers in coloured crayon, one made up of two figures and the other by five figures, no doubt written by the shopkeeper who had sold it. I tried to erase the five-figure number since it was too visible on the upper part of the arm. While making the object I noticed that the remaining number was 22. This funereal number that had appeared with such necessity seemed to me, through a causality linking it to objective chance, to be a worrying unknown quantity whose mathematical solution perhaps hid a magical agency. The diabolically unconscious intervention of the shopkeeper in this mechanism of desire, and above all the role played by his filing system in the determination of chance, cast such an obscure and obscuring gap between causality and necessity that only a mathematical exploration of obscurity could hope to find its way in this morass of numbers.

Despite the magical obscurantism of this causal determination, the necessity of the number 22 was revealed as a diamond in a forest night. The funereal number 22 appeared as an object with a satisfied (although forbidden) erotic function.[12] The feelings of guilt to which masturbation is always tied imposed the apparition of the number 22.

While I was making *Dusk* and discovering the presence of the number 22, I learned that Victor Brauner's father had died. His natural death (after a long and painful illness, as they say in obituaries) now no longer seemed so "natural." If several determining factors came into play in his death, one was criminal in nature. The exchange of masturbatory objects grafted onto the Oedipus complex here gained a power of enchantment capable of provoking or hastening the father's death. From being in a passive and determined state, the feeling of guilt moved towards an active and determining role. The number 22 written on *Dusk* was a mortal poison.

The Ideal Phantom (G.)
The Statue of the Libido (Hélène)
The "No" (V.)

The materials I use in making objects have never been imposed upon me by their substance. The fact that the woman in *The Letter L* was neither living nor dead did not pose an obstacle in the unravelling of its phenomena. In a world in which symbols have the emotive power of actions and agents, in which for the first time living bodies gain their freedom to live within their shadows, which are more alive and more real than bodies, the materials from which I construct objects can be made of paper or celluloid. In the world of dreams where I choose to operate, celluloid is flesh and paper is water.

On 9 November 1940, objects could only be made of gold. At the time I could not understand why this substance in particular imposed itself upon me, but I felt an infinite regret in lacking the money needed to buy a few kilos of gold with which to make these objects. I substituted bronze instead.

The Statue of the Libido (fig. 12) was a contraption with two long handles, one of which was moveable and ended in a disk that could cover the opening of the cylinder. At the bottom of this cylinder, on black velvet, lay several sodomised children. A black revolver was attached to the second handle.

The Ideal Phantom (fig. 11) was a metallic head with two eye-breasts, resembling a drawing by Magritte. A negative nose went down below the eyes, on which the maker's name "Ideal" was written. The lower part of the head ended in a horizontal circular opening, like a chin. A rod with a spring ran through the head and penetrated the opening every time the loop fixed on top of the tube was pressed.

The "No" was a concave porcelain plate (gilded, naturally) in the middle of which was placed the photograph of a woman lifting up her dress, cut out in a circle. A ball bearing could run in a circle around the rim of the plate. Once the plate was still, the ball rolled into the centre of the plate and stopped under the woman's dress.

I finished my work at 1 a.m. and put the objects near the fireplace. Slipping into bed, I was afraid to fall asleep because I had the premonition that there would be an earthquake that night.

I was awoken at 4 a.m. by a dreadful earthquake: the walls were shaking, wardrobes flung across the room, books falling down on all sides, objects and glasses smashing.[13] Throughout the duration of the quake I kept shouting that I knew it would happen. These powers of prediction, which

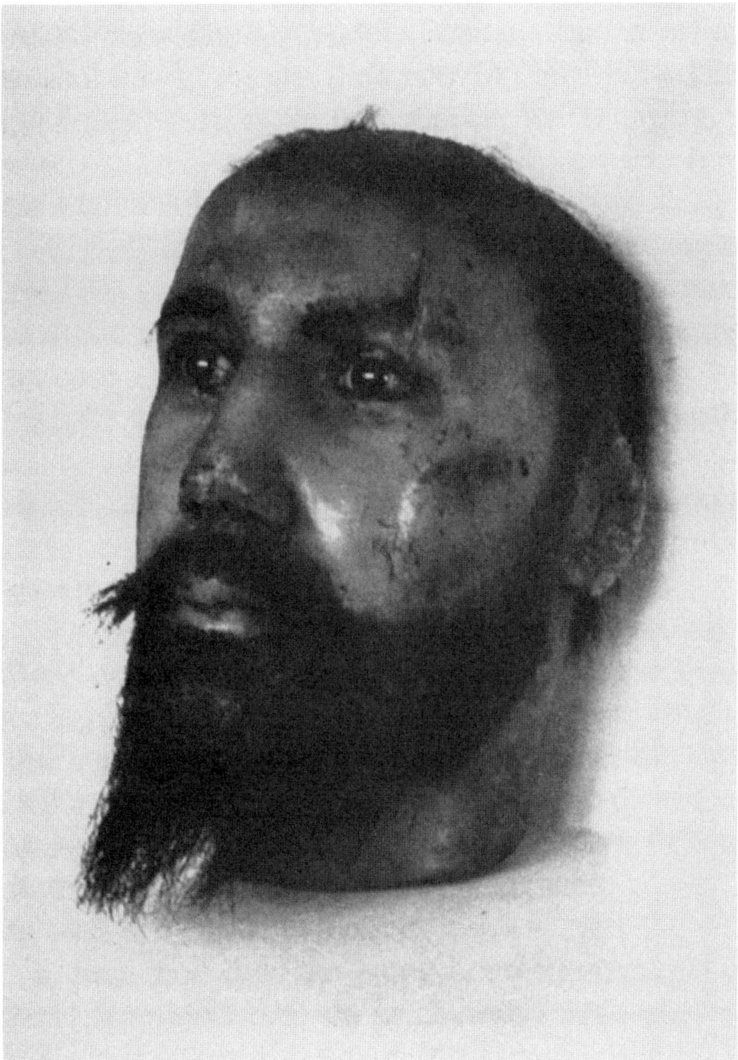

Fig. 5 Clairvoyance in Varying Degrees

I was discovering for the first time, only increased my terror. Half an hour later G. came over from the other side of town to see if I had survived, and told me the city was in ruins. I gave him *The Ideal Phantom*, and we went outside. The streets were full of destruction and rubble, and this town I'd never liked, with its stupid people, stupid streets, and stupid houses, was now unrecognisable, now it had a truly unique beauty, and scantily-clad women traversed it like ghosts.* A twelve-storey building in the city centre had totally collapsed. Caught up in her bed sheets, a woman who had fallen from the top floor found herself alive and alone on the pavement. Her husband had been thrown out of bed. From now on she would sleep forever, since reality was now as extraordinary as dreams. I listened to people recounting their reactions to each other and returned home to take the following notes:

During, or else immediately after, the earthquake, either the sole or the first human erotic desire is to masturbate. Such an experience, awakening the instinct of self-preservation in

* "They are the nocturnal visitors who rouse children and take them up to prevent their wetting their beds, or who lift the bedclothes to make sure where they have put their hands in their sleep. Analyses of some of these anxiety-dreams have made it possible for me to identify these nocturnal visitors more precisely. In every case the robbers stood for the sleeper's father, whereas the ghosts corresponded to female figures in white nightgowns" (*The Interpretation of Dreams*).[14]

such an extreme and contracted form within each individual, means that in response those sexual impulses which normally accompany the instinct in all their complexity now became simplified. The supreme defence of one's own being in the most terrifying moment of panic can only be followed by an erotic release in the form of auto-eroticism.

This explanation is accompanied by the enormous excitation provoked in the unconscious by infantile rocking motions. When describing their experiences during the earthquake, almost everyone spoke about the rocking of objects – and above all of light fixtures – with a masturbatory hand gesture. The desire to masturbate was being satisfied by this symptomatic action in each account.

Two years earlier, during a conversation with my friends in Paris, I had claimed that I would find great satisfaction in a major catastrophe – the destruction of the Earth by a comet, for example, as foretold by astronomers. In a time of violent revolutionary pessimism, like that during which this conversation took place, several weeks after France's entry into the war, it seemed justifiable to exchange one desperate but vital solution for another that was so natural yet so alien to us. At the level of desire, such a catastrophe being predicted in advance would have offered me, hastily and for a limited time, the satisfactions a revolutionary transformation of the world would have given me over a whole lifetime.*

The irrational construction of the three bronze objects was the lyrical representation of our rational debate from two years earlier. That which twenty-four hours before the catastrophe had occupied the unconscious zone of the psychic mechanism had become conscious three hours before it struck. At 1 a.m. I foresaw the catastrophe that would take place at 4 a.m. because only at that moment did the panic-desire to satisfy all my desires through panic make its way into consciousness via the irrationality of the objects, and the subterranean events being communicated to me by the mountains hundreds of miles away thus corresponded to the shadowy psychic events that I was communicating to the objects.

* It was G., who was party to our conversation and who disagreed with me, who came to find me two years later straight after the earthquake to tell me that the city was truly extraordinary and that a walk across it would provide us with a splendid spectacle. Obviously, the desire to find me dead was the primary explanation of his visit, but at the same time, it was also an acceptance of my argument in Paris. The desire for a catastrophe had made its way between us and, emerging from the ruins like a phantom, G. had come straight to my door, even though he lived on the other side of town, to take *The Ideal Phantom,* an object of disintegration and instant satisfactions. He had come to make sure where I had put my hands, but at the same time I could make sure where he had put his. So we were both ideal phantoms, since we had appeared in the night not to prevent a forbidden erotic practice, but to acknowledge it in each other.

Only the most malicious rationalists or short-sighted positivists would claim that this mysterious communication between two shadows (since I will never accept that the unknown centre of our planet is greater than the one within us all, or that the surveys conducted by geologists under the Earth's crust go deeper than those by Hegel, Engels, Freud, and Breton into humanity) approaches mysticism. To attribute it to coincidence, or to seek comforting answers for any of its obscurity in medical science based on the telepathic powers of hypothesis or hysteria seems to me to be a convenient and pseudoscientific response that is much closer to mysticism than the attempt to verify – from humankind all the way out to the cosmos – the correspondences provoked by objective chance in the relationships between people, between people and objects, between people and their history.

The panic-desire to satisfy all my desires through panic, substituted for my perpetual desire to change the world through revolution, met the external causality of the earthquake at the heart of the mountains, and the objects I had irrationally created several hours beforehand took their place in my consciousness in the form of a prediction of a catastrophe, which I had wished for and participated in.

Making the objects in bronze or in gold seemed necessary

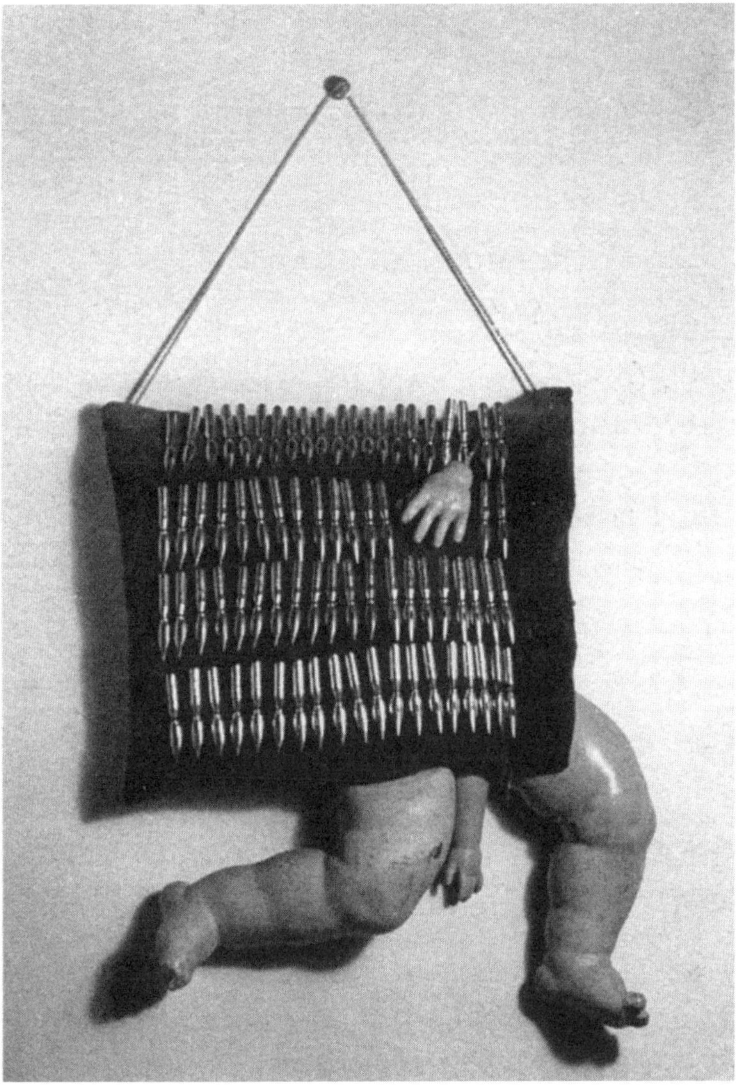

Fig. 6 Dusk

to me because it is only vases and statuettes made of these resilient materials that archaeologists find beneath ruins. A distance of several thousand years lay between me and the objects I was making. I invented and discovered them at the same time, I buried them and dug them up simultaneously on the delirious scale of space and time. We are both living and fossilised, like a hand on an x-ray plate.

These objects made out of bronze belonged to the earthquake. One had a spring-loaded rod, the other its moveable handle, and the third had its ball bearing moving at a constant distance around the rim of the plate. These were masturbatory objects through which erotic narcissism accompanied the narcissism of the instinct for self-preservation. In the splendid rocking of the earthquake, humanity was masturbating with these objects. The woman who had fallen from the twelfth floor and found herself alive and well on the pavement could do without her husband, who remained suspended somewhere high in the air, or on a beam of the disintegrated building. Those who survived were telling each other breathlessly of their sensations during the catastrophe, and one could read an unbearable satisfaction on their faces. They were still living with the sensations of the supreme rocking that had all of a sudden thrown them into the shadows of their childhood and of humanity. They masturbated themselves furiously, desperately, angelically, eyes wide open onto the walls, wrapped in swaddling clothes. Now they were two years old, now just a year old, they disappeared, they huddled up in a humid warmth, in the impenetrable darkness of their mothers' bellies. The panic-desire to provoke an earthquake, through which the never-ending desire for revolution was making its way, was the point towards which my great, my supreme desire to regain my mother's womb was destined.

The sodomised children at the bottom of the cylinder (*The Statue of the Libido*) were making love, on their own or in pairs, on a piece of black velvet: a forbidden and nostalgic love. So long as the Earth continued to turn without being turned upside-down by revolutionary change throughout the world, the ball bearing too (*The "No"*) would trace its pathetic orbit at a constant distance from the object it so desired. A catastrophe happens – the desperate form revolution takes at the level of desire – and the ball heads for the middle of the plate where the welcoming interior of a woman awaits.

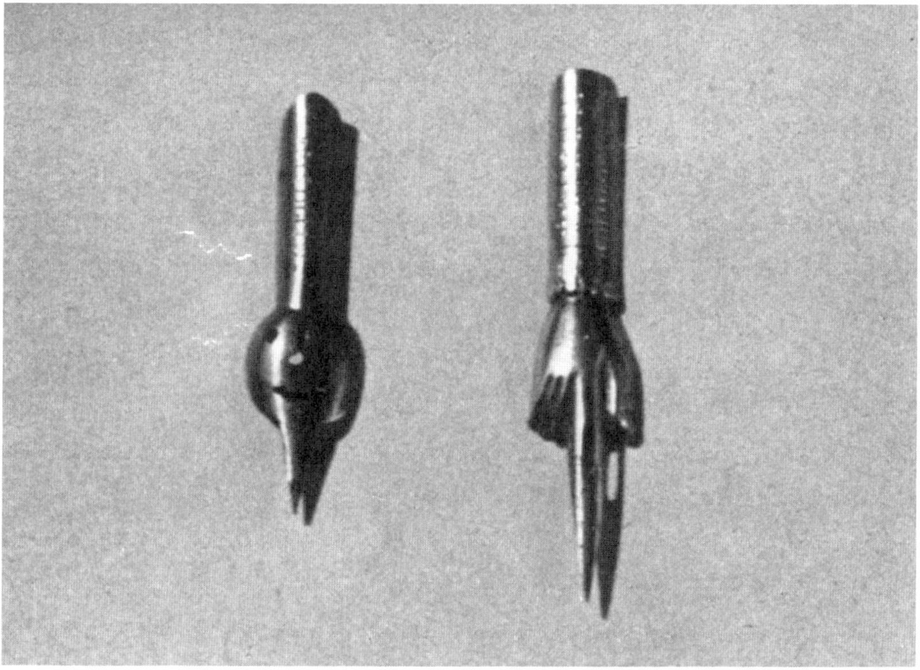

Fig. 7 Pills for Dreams

THE PASSIVE VAMPIRE

Objects, these mysterious suits of armour beneath which desire awaits us, nocturnal and laid bare, these snares made of velvet, of bronze, of gossamer that we throw at ourselves with each step we take; hunter and prey in the shadows of forests, at once forest, poacher, and woodcutter, that woodcutter killed at the foot of a tree and covered with his own beard smelling of incense, of well-being, and of the that's-not-possible; free at last, alone at last with ourselves and with everyone else, advancing in the darkness with feline eyes, with jackals' teeth, with hair in lyrical, tousled ringlets, beneath a shirt of veins and arteries through which the blood flows for the first time, we're lit up inside ourselves by the giant spotlights of the very first gesture, saying what must be said, doing what must be done, led among the lianas, butterflies, and bats, like the black and white on a chessboard; no one would dream of forbidding the black squares and the bishop – the ants vanish, the king and queen vanish, the alarm clocks vanish in turn, we reintroduce the walking stick, the bicycle with odd wheels, the timepiece, the airship, keeping the siphon, the telephone receiver, the shower head, the lift, the syringe, the automatic mechanisms that deliver chocolate when numbered buttons are pressed; objects, this catalepsy, this steady spasm, this "stream one never steps in twice" and into which we plunge as into a photograph; objects, those philosopher's stones that discover, transform, hallucinate, communicate our screaming, those stone-screams that break the waves, through which the rainbow, living images, images of the image will pass, I dream of you because I dream of myself, hypnotically I aim at the diamond contained within you, before falling asleep, before you fall asleep, we pass through each other like two ghosts in a marble room whose walls are hung with life-sized portraits of our ancestors, with the portrait of a mediaeval knight next to the portrait of a chair* gazing at the two fossils of ghosts on the walls of this spectral museum, and if it is true that we are shadows, then the people and the objects all around us here are nothing but the bones of shadows, the shadows of shadows, since here they don't die, here

* In a hypnotism manual I saw the portrait of a woman in a cataleptic trance holding a chair in an unaccustomed position, and to me the portrait was at the same time one of a chair holding a woman in an unaccustomed position.

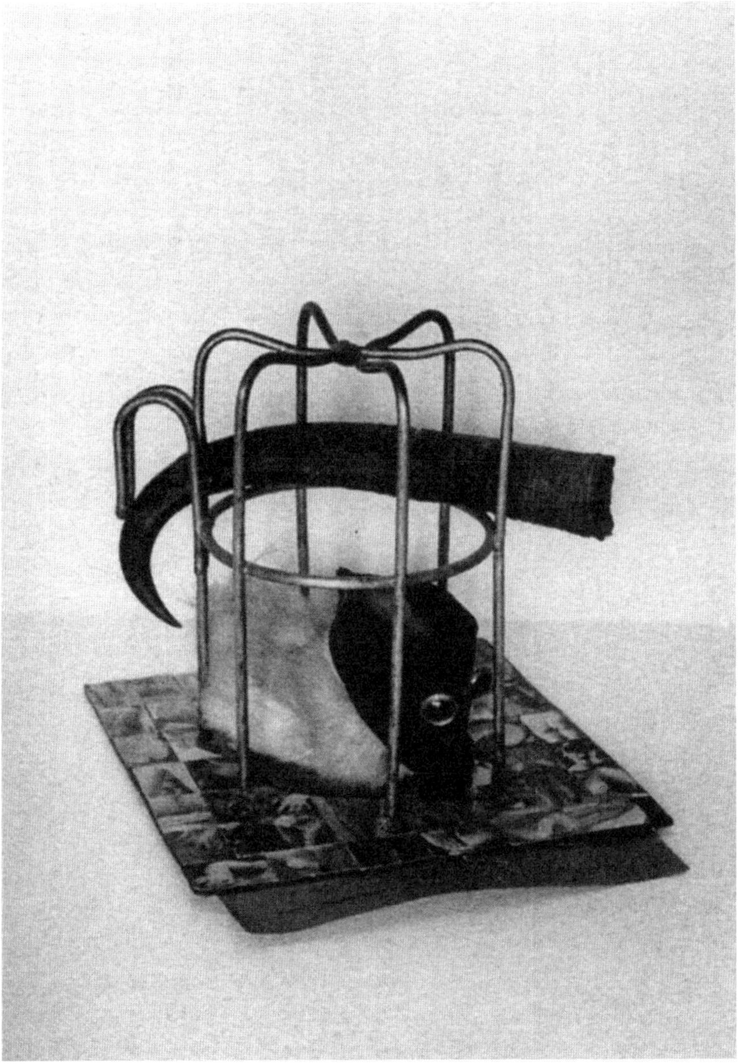

Fig. 8 Latent Powers Considered as Possibilities

the passing, removal, or putrefaction of a woman is not enough to kill the desire connected to her, like the flame of a candle to the play of shadow and light it maintains around it, when, trembling between the sheets and transfigured by fever, one murmurs her beloved name; no, as long as desire persists there is no death: the living die more easily, these men I meet in the street making the usual gestures, smiling or furrowing their brows on the café terraces or on the metro, hurrying, wearing hats, wearing ears. These men have been dead for a long time, even if they've never been born – as for my father, I killed him before he died, while my mother still isn't dead, even if they tell me she is, and even if a brain in braces and a flour heart make me realise that I don't know the frontier between desire and reality, I'll remind them about dream, I'll remind them of the reality of desire's tomorrow or, perhaps, I'll insult them and, while I keep looking at the portraits on the walls, it's with *pleasure* that I'll confuse the chair with a mediaeval knight, the shoe with the wan marquise who is slipping it on. I'll walk into the next room arm in arm with the object, between shadows and their fossils, between the mirrors that don't reflect me, between the looks that don't spy me, that don't dissect me, unable to surprise anything and with nothing apt to surprise me in a world of surprise, in a world of unexpected apparitions, which I expect even while not expecting them; they reveal themselves before being expected, at the precise moment when the lips get moistened to receive the kiss or else the teeth or else the wind or else the white neck revealing itself to the moon, offering itself to the cold breaths (like two stilettos) of the vampire. Here we are in the final chamber, O object! Let's take the stairs that lead us down into the castle's caverns, let's lose our way among all these long corridors and distant calls like a great river seen from its mouth upstream, let's walk gingerly so as not to stir the stones' dust, the molecules' soot, and let's leave the huge spider webs untouched, adopting their terrible owners' fascinating acrobatics, and I'll offer the object a spider just as I offer the bed a woman who offers herself to me. I offer the object to other objects in the same way that images encounter one another in poems and dreams, since the object offered objectively to an object (O.O.O.O.) is a magical process of communication between the ego and the id, whereby for a given moment the object is divested of its nature as a mediating symbol in erotic practices (like poems, dreams, daydreams, games of exquisite corpse,[15] or collages), putting us in the delirious state of fetish worshippers in which the symbol supersedes the thing it symbolises – for me the lover who puts a flower in his beloved's hair or pours champagne into her dancing shoes typifies a lover offering objects to other objects. This magical process of communication gives us the possibility to move about more freely in a world of apparitions, which more closely corresponds to who we are and denies the reality-obstacle through the simple process of clasping a shadow. In this world of apparitions, shadows become flesh, they can be loved and photographed like the phenomenon of the split personality found in clairvoyance.

In this universe of phantoms, I feel as if encircled by fire, as if in one of those set pieces where the Devil is invoked. All I need is to look at my palm spread before me in the semi-darkness to see, as though on a screen or on the disconcerting surface of an aquarium, a luminous and shadowy aura, from which a woman's hair emerges like a handful of ashes cast onto the retina. I know that beyond my palm the profile of this woman is cut into a diamond and that I only need move one finger to see her mortal pallor. But in front of me, on a chair, a cape beneath which someone is breathing tells me that I am not alone. And in my lap rises up another apparition, like a statue made of water, her breasts bared, her shoulders glass. The gestures I manage to make are so simple and basic that I have the impression I am moving through a world that is not solely a realm of conjecture. I cannot understand how, beyond the window, in the street, in their homes, people can still live in discord with themselves. How can it be that the mechanisms for nocturnal recording are rejected the following morning, and that when, rent and disfigured by their own contradictions, people are forced back to these mechanisms, nothing has been altered in the order of things?

I can no longer say that I'm dreaming; the hundreds of thousands of years of dreams are enough for me, and if the castaway's message in a bottle floats on the waters, then somewhere, eventually, a shore awaits it. I have deciphered this sign that has risen from the darkness, and to feign amnesia during the daytime would be to hide from my own shadow. The world I move in during the day does not contradict the one that exists at night. This is why I cannot claim to be troubled by the fact that humanity only lives half of the time. I no longer say that I dream, because the quantitative difference between the two phenomena of day and night also implies a qualitative one.

I would propose the discovery of a new language that genuinely expresses the psychic phenomena which resemble, but are not identical to, dream. This dream which, even if still opposed to external reality, has long since ceased to

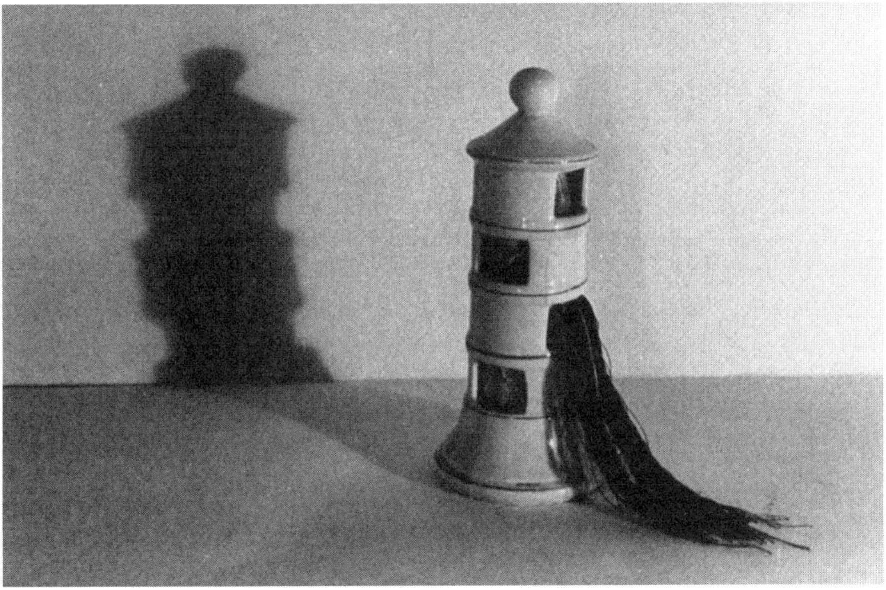

Fig. 9 Astrological Birth Chart

be opposed to the life of the dreamer. In this language, the one I have been unable to find, the ancient antinomies, beginning with that of good and evil, will be resolved for the meanwhile at an individual level. The surrealists – who at this individual level represent synthesis – have found a way out of that great drama separating the dreamer from the dream, while on a collective level their coming to consciousness still holds them within this drama. The nocturnal image, which in its waking state finds its identity in the apparition of phantoms, leads us to consider people and objects with no psychic resonance as equivalent to the diurnal residue of the dream. We approach the world of phantoms as we would a reality lying outside this world at odds with itself, a world with no valid correspondence within ourselves. In the world in which I like to breathe, a box can take on the same psychic content of a beloved woman; the delirious and fetishistic love between a man and a box thus casts a prophetic, thaumaturgic light onto the outer world. Because of the multiple possibilities for symbolisation that an impulse might assume, tomorrow's world will be given a quality that corresponds to our inner delirium. Phantoms will be approachable and commonplace, and we will no longer need the pretentious rituals of hypnotic séances to produce mediumistic phenomena; in a world where the mediumistic will be commonplace, the projecting of our unconscious will occcur as automatically as a slip of the tongue. A man smitten with a shoe will no longer be exposed in journals of psychiatry – those revolting prisons in which our society reveals its own monstrosity by seeking to put its "monsters" on display – and the nimbused phantoms of paralytic spirits will transform their haloes into spittoons and gather around us to complete our dreams, our poems, our simplest gestures.

How many times have I thought of you, you hair-worshipper, standing at the Trocadéro metro station at six in the evening with a pair of scissors sticking from your hand like an erection, waiting for schoolgirls with their long plaits? Why do these scissors and the tresses hidden under your shirt make me think of that place of the chance encounter in *Maldoror,* the dissecting table?[16] Why this woman-object (fig. 13) with a heart like an icy shred of ectoplasm, with her diaphanous skin through which the wind blows and pipettes full of milk from passive vampires pass. Why put this solid shadow on a dissecting table as though at the feet of the most superb woman?

How otherwise could I reveal the sadomasochistic confusion lying at the depths of my active and passive being, like the idea of a wound, provocative and provoked like the whiteness that springs from a solar spectre? And my great, my supreme desire to spill blood, to dive into a bath of blood, to drink blood, to breathe blood, how could I understand this desire without the sacrifice of blood which I am ready to make?* And the ever more ample, ever more shadowy maternal breast that with mathematical exactitude directs each of our gestures, how much closer does it get to us with each drop of blood shed? And that handsome vampire, paler than a letter, eyes closed, the tresses of mist flung around his shoulders, flung around his sword, sucks in frenzy. His leaps forward and back are made in solitude, like a block of ice, foretelling the past, revealing the future, casting onto the world a spectral light, a tenebrous light.

I close my eyes, as active as a vampire, I open them within myself, as passive as a vampire, and between the blood that arrives, the blood that leaves, and the blood already inside me there occurs an exchange of images like an engagement of daggers. Now I could eat a piano, shoot a table, inhale a staircase. All the extremities of my body have orifices out of which come the skeletons of the piano, the table, the staircase, and for the very first time these ordinary – and therefore non-existent – objects can exist. I climb this

* "When atheism will wish for martyrs, let it designate them, my blood is ready to be shed" (Sade).[17]

staircase not to get to the first floor but to get closer to myself. I lean on the banisters not to avoid vertigo but to prolong it. If when I get to the top floor I open a door that leads straight out onto the street, I will fall into space but will not die. If I do happen to die, it is a phenomenon used by another objective and more easily understandable phenomenon only as a pretext. I understand the feeling of guilt but I do not understand death. I am unable to understand how this iniquity, this error, has led to the extermination of so many generations and how humankind can treat it as a finality (and I'm not referring to those swine who talk about the afterlife). Death is an irremediable end, a "truth," an ultimate obstacle among the reality of obstacles. Within this reality, in which the elixir of life is a fantasy, an alchemist's dream, death is irremediable, definitive. For us, the alchemists' dream, like any dream, is a part of reality. We deny false external reality, we deny the false reality of death, we deny all repression. The elixir of life is a prophetic dream, and if we think of the reality of desire, then all dreams should be considered prophetic. At worst tomorrow's death will be a macabre substitute for pleasure, a traumatic remnant bequeathed by past generations that keeps up the impulses' play of shadow and light, yet physical, irremediable, definitive death will be nothing but a sinister utopia. In

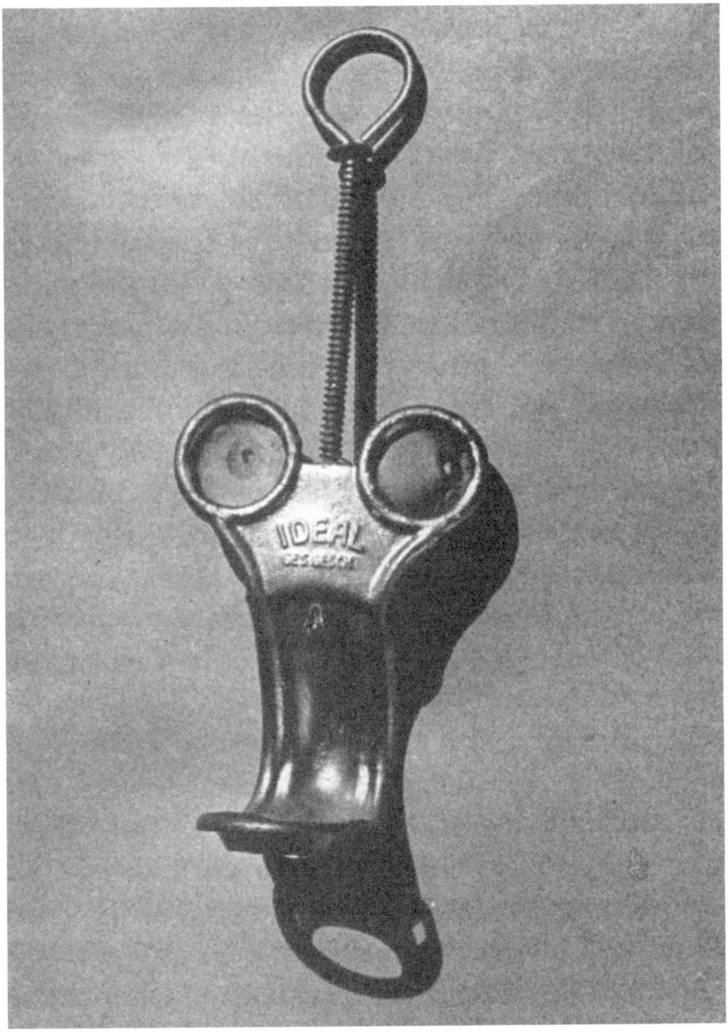

Fig. 11 The Ideal Phantom

today's society, only those with the psychology of a corpse can talk naively about a "natural" death.

Since I've started living out my dreams, since I've become the contemporary of the centuries to come, I no longer know death under the annihilating guise it has maintained in today's society. Only in my moments of deepest depression do I realise that in that world of swine into which I was born I shall be forced to die, just as out in the street I'm obliged to rub shoulders with priests and cops.

But the deepest moments of depression cannot conquer my life. Beyond these deceptive troughs into which I sometimes fall, my nocturnal and diurnal life is real. Here death, in order to become a real phenomenon, seeks libidinal equivalents, and it is only in this new guise that it can exercise some function in our psychic apparatus. Just as the unobtrusive and anonymous Fantômas[18] can only become the Master of Terror, the Criminal Genius, the Executioner when he dons his tight black outfit and hood, I would like to be a killer in a white velvet costume, at an operating table or leaning over a child's pram. At another operating table, by the window whose open curtains let in the rays of moonlight, stands the handsome, silent vampire. In evening dress, his lips glued to a bared neck like a bird, now he resembles a flautist playing pulses of blood on living instruments. At slightly increasing intervals the drops flow from the instrument to his lips. Each gulp is held for a while in his mouth to let the scent reach his nostrils, to intoxicate his breath. Like a fiery whip across the breast, the drink passes swiftly through the digestive system. Tottering, growing increasingly pale, ever more solitary, the handsome vampire swallows another gulp of blood. Dressed in white velvet, I'd like to vivisect a child, from time to time looking up at the vampire by the window, moonlight streaking his face.

Dreadful negations of death; crime, like all phantoms, emerges from the darkness. With a ray as bright as lightning, the black flash of murder tears open the shadows by illuminating them from within, like an owl's eye. On the knife blade our advance seems so natural that the great causeways traversing the continents appear to us like treacherous traps. Immense slabs of basalt slip from the crusts of mountains, of trees, of voices. On them we read: No! Exhausted waterfowl spring from men's ears towards the four points of the compass. I don't know if the sparrow-hawk lying in wait for them is actually a duck or if their ears are now wild capital letters, howling furiously at the moon. There is one moon in the firmament and another in pictures. Between the two every form of love, known and unknown, reveals and invents itself. The fibers of a watch stopped at midnight and the fibers of a whale drowned in the Pacific spin in the dark an aluminium net for trawling for cathedrals. What symmetrically bundled-up birds these cathedrals are, oranges ready for export, traditional as the notion of sin! A basket of bread stretched out over the landscape so as to turn the edible symbol into a monument. The horses bolt from between the riders' legs and jump up onto the plinths. Refusing to be a pedestrian is as impressive as a wounded vulture. But to be obliged to find your own torn-off testicles in every city square the world over is an atrocity greater than a boat. I refuse all forms, all categories, all acts, all plans, all laws, all your castrating scents. I eat, breathe, drink, think, reject, dress myself and move *aphrodisiacally*. I keep every cell of my being in a state of permanent excitation, excited and exciting at the same time, the zones traversing my being are genital and pregenital, erotic and criminal, black, ferocious, satanic. If in order to appear to the mediaeval sorcerer's imagination the Devil requested that he separate himself from the world by using a circle of fire immune to human stupidity, now the protection of a circle is no longer needed for the Devil to show himself. Man, so that he might live out his own being, will no longer need to hide in sleep as in a ring of fire. He will move through sleep as he moves through waking, without knowing if he is asleep or awake. The flames will be triangular, their angles opening onto infinity, and between their limitless edges man will live out his own being for the very first time.

"Lord of misrule, Dispenser of the spoils of crime, Custodian of luxurious sins and great vices, Satan, it is you we adore, logical God, just God."[19]

This cry, sprung from the depths of black masses, feels more appropriate on my lips than ever now that the bourgeoisie sends its armies blessed by priests into battle, now that sleep is nothing but the modern and aggressive form of invoking the Devil. And if their cry, which I feel burning within me, convulses me wildly, ushering me into the great hidden truths at the heart of humanity, I furiously shout out the same obscurantist and prophetic cries to the Creator:

"Monster, you whose inconceivable ferocity shall engender the life it will inflict on those innocent beings you dare condemn in the name of who knows what original sin, those you dare punish in the name of who knows which laws, we nevertheless demand you confess your impudent lies, your inexpiable crimes! We wish to hammer in your

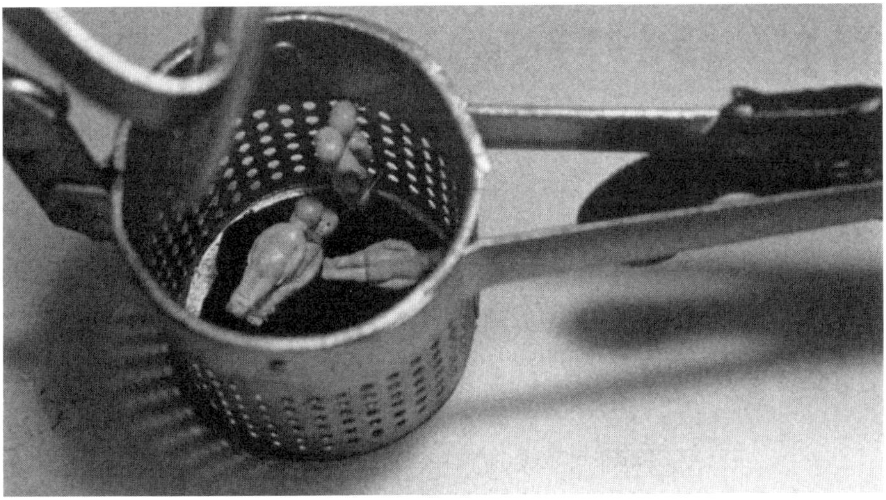

Fig. 12 The Statue of the Libido

nails, twist your thorns, see the blood of your suffering flowing again around your congealed wounds! These things we can and we will do, violating the peace of your body, Profaner of profuse vices, Abstractor of idiotic purities, cursed Nazarene, useless King, cowardly God!"

The pyres of the Middle Ages are still burning. Workers, poets, thinkers all carry on the magician's work. With each newly discovered truth we sign a pact with Satan. The signatures of these enlightened dreamers, made in blood on parchment, we now write by the hundreds of thousands on the cobblestones, on prison walls. Every dream, every act of love, every riot is a black mass.

"And the Flesh was made Word. For it was decreed that we shall be saved by flesh: we must walk naked through life and destroy Evil through Evil, by our frenzied abandon to it."

The dreamer, the lover, the revolutionary are all unknowingly committing demonic acts. For, whatever your name: Sammael, Phiton, Asmodeus, Lucifer, Belial, Beelzebub, Satan,* we shall only recognize you, O Demon, in our valid actions and ideas.

* Lucifer = he who brings light
Belial = he who rejects the yoke or utility
Beelzebub = Lord of the flies
Satan = the adversary.

Only our just actions and ideas have the infernal capacity to unleash panic and terror, love, hate, the real functioning of thought, geological upheavals. They alone, a fistful of dynamite, move among people like a phosphorus eye. An unbearable dread can be seen on people's dazed faces, in their absurd frozen gestures, as though they had witnessed some dreadful catastrophe, as though they had been buried alive at the foot of an erupting volcano. It is dawning on them at last that they have long since ceased to live, that the corpses they show to the outside world, having taken the form of the useful, the beautiful, and the good, have transformed the magnificent rotation of the Earth around the Sun into the funereal procession of a slowly decaying hearse as it approaches the ruins of a cemetery.

Young demon, I can hear your legendary laugh smash into the four horizons and the four dimensions. Each blow struck by your outburst, like a corroded pearl, sets in motion an unknown mechanism buried in the living vaults of humanity as though in a bath of blood. The primordial poisons fill the communicating vessel linking us to the outer world, and their bitter gall makes our blood aphrodisiac, thins our fingernails to a thread that ties us to objects and to shadows, heaving onto our shoulders amphorae in which women bathe; in the forests where butterflies, jackals, and flaming squirrels are lovers, the eye, turned into a prism with all its faces in spasm, leads us like a horse through a universe of ashes.

Adopting the simple sign of the mediaeval visionaries, I sign a pact with Satan in my own blood (fig. 14) in the event my poems and actions might not be proof enough of the indestructible love that binds me to the Demon. This pact, which I place in a lamp full of smoke, a vice lamp, and in which I can see no other mission than that of *Love,* will lend the century in which I have had the misfortune to be born something of the dazzling obscurity of past centuries, something of the pearlescent pallor of the centuries to come.

But the blood with which I sign this pact ceased to belong to me long ago. It has been completely given over to the Demon, in the encounter with the first repression, in the first that's-not-allowed, when I signed this dreadful gift of blood, even if I was still ignorant of the signs and articulate language of humankind, knowing only the fundamental language of desire when, with my evaporated eyes and my lips like a suction cup, I first breathed in the warmth of the maternal breast as though under a cloak of flames cast over me by the sublime angels of the shadows.

A system of levers, built using the same system as the apple attached to William Tell's arrow, displaces objects from one eddy to another, from one mist to another, and a bitter vertigo settles on our cells like a glass of poison downed in one gulp. My brow marked with blood, I advance through this forest of objects, my clothes, skin, muscles, and wings torn by their cruel angles, and beneath my feet that tread as though on a gaping wound I feel the slow, damp slip of the earth, the slip of a toad.

At last I have found the paths of blood and poison along which I must advance, and on the horizon, like a magnificent scarecrow with goat's wings and an angel's sabots, the Genie, the Prince of Darkness awaits me. Now that my fingernails are ten steel knives, now that my lips are colder, thinner and sharper than their mortal blades, now that with a single glance I can wither a whole plantation, now that with my breath alone I can induce monstrous epidemics, these paths I take could be internal as much as external, just like reflections on velvet.

I know who really sends the poisoned flowers (fig. 15), poisoned letters and sweets as homage to a beloved, and no image could suggest the love of these fierce worshippers to me, save perhaps the figure carved from a block of coal of the legendary Gilles de Rais, stroking a child with one hand

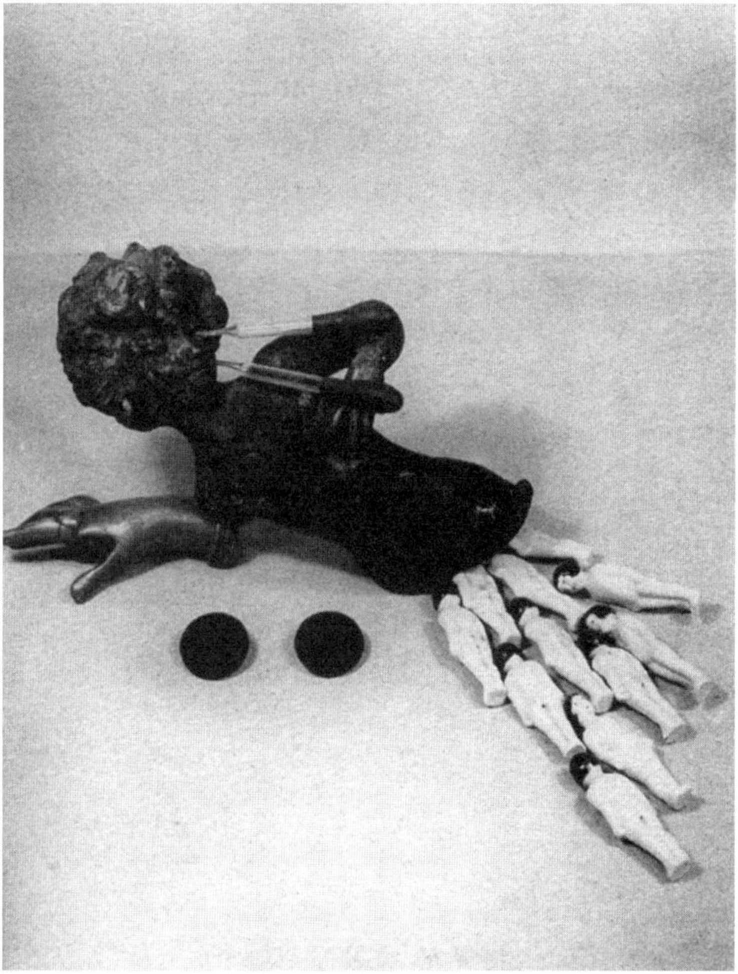

Fig. 13 The Passive Vampire

while he slits its throat with the other. The case of Rose Keller, as we know her from biographies of the Divine Marquis, might also throw a revealing light on these fabulous supplies of objects. Wrenched from the mundanity of conventionalised gifts, by way of the delirious vegetation of Des Esseintes's room, the flowers that, in exchange for their perfume, have been sprayed with a bottle of poison might become, in the arms of the beloved, a bouquet of impulses, a black chart of desire.[20] How feeble, how pale and artificial the image of that sentimental exchange of poisoned kisses on Juliet's tomb seems in the light of these ferociously offered flowers. An idealist maggot destroys all those gestures of today's lovers descended from Romeo and Juliet, that sinister pair presented to us as a model couple. An acid stain thrown onto their lives disfigures their transports, lays waste to their plans, and drives them like trained machines towards ready-made images, towards permitted images. The nature of the flowers one gives, which change in florists' windows and lovers' arms according to the seasons, offers us nothing but an external spectacle like someone opening an umbrella when it rains. The artificial flowers carried artificially in a lover's arms are laid at the feet of the beloved so that the artificial society in which we live might prolong its death throes.

Poisoned flowers, these flowers which could be vultures or fingers or sea horses and which are always wild mirrors born from our bodies, with the Devil's eye cast onto them like an imprint, like a thunderstorm, pass from our blood into that of our beloved crossing the shadows. A fantastic flora, virgin and demented, the faithful image of that terrible fauna from the heart of our being. A carnivorous plant ten times larger than a man that I send to my beloved and that is returned to me the next day with its petals a little bit heavier and its leaves tinged with red. The pleasure of receiving a branch of cherry blossoms from which hangs a wounded magpie. Or perhaps a huge leather-bound herbarium crawling with lice. Water lilies floating in a bowl of sperm. A severed breast, to it pinned a rose. A carnation in a basket of blind cats. A tulip furnished with a silver trap. A bouquet of lilies reeking of sweat. A field of daisies put through a printing press. A hypnotised sunflower. A white violet. An orchid from which dangle long black strands of a woman's hair and onto which fall smaller orchids and shorter hairs just as black. Secret herbs, hellish tasting plants, roots resembling monsters are torn from the soil and secretly placed in garrets and laboratories at nightfall. After removing their shadows and their soot, after violating the locks that secured them one by one, they are transformed

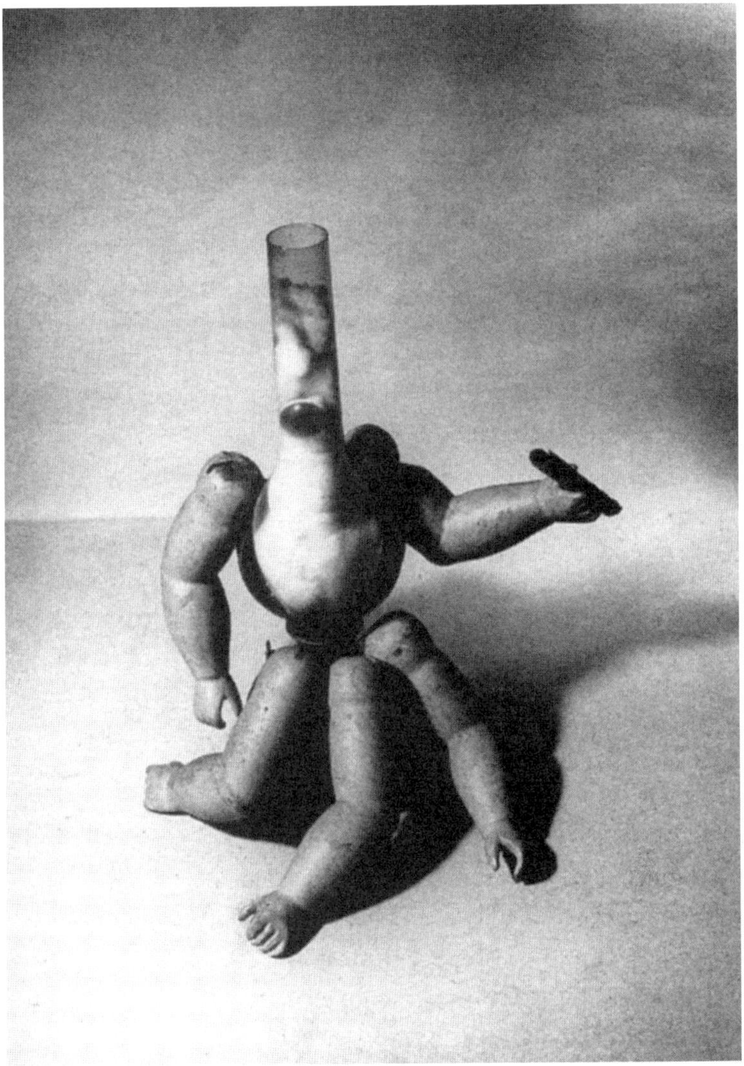

Fig. 14 Black Love

here into magic powder, into revelatory images, destined to maintain humankind's fascinating oscillation between love and hate at a temperature equal to that of fire. At a temperature permanently equal to that of fire, love and hate meet and intersect like two gunshots fired from a distance. Leaning over the burning retorts, the lyric-magician thrusts the full length of his arms into the man's chest, and with his hands, their shrivelling skin, the fingernails torn away, he holds steady the burning centre, this double-edged heart, this wild bird of night whose eyes alone are to be seen. Macabre cuisine, powerful aphrodisiacs, a jar of spiders, a spoonful of mandrake, and far away a woman's heart begins beating for me like a river. I can feel its swift waters bathing the universe, a web of seaweed, a net of bats cleaving our destinies together to a slender, delirious wire. Almighty love, which finds its raison d'être in the violent hatred that reflects it like an ocean, now has the span, depth, and wild roar of the ocean. With the passion of a collector, I save little bits of nail clippings, single hairs found on a dress, linen with the fresh smell of sweat, mistakes, interrupted images, fragments of dreams recounted by my beloved, incomprehensible gestures. In the darkest corner of my room, beneath the unlit oven and a wild root, the lyric-magician looks at a wax figure through dark-ringed eyes. All the cold poisons he can sense within himself, like a shirt of ether, all the frozen fires that set his breath alight, snorting lacerating shards of ash from his nostrils, has made him resemble the infernal object he has in front of him, like two bite marks, like two shadows. With the same pallor the wax doll, through which he sends the faint trace of marsh alongside the trace of a thin vein, awaits the tender caress and the skilful torture. Several miles away the beloved feels her flesh riven with desires or torn by a wild atrocity, a hand in a velvet glove sliding a sperm of silk or sulphur down her thighs. At the hour of cockcrow, when night hangs over the city by a single thread, the lyric-magician closes his four-bladed knife and restores a black torpor to the room around him, like a field leaning against a shoulder. Behind him, the image of the beloved, who hasn't lost a single drop of her blood, intoxicated by the echo of distant flesh, lost on the marital bed whose taste is just a bitter shadow, lies in the darkest corner of the room, a poisoned flower tossed between an owl and a wild root.

Here (fig. 16) is the magic hothouse towards which the lover directs his somnambulant steps, an enormous partridge on each shoulder. A surgical, mathematical hand pulls up the flower whose roots are thrust deep into love and, like a floating cape, its scent opens the beloved's lungs with a lancet. The oneiric image projects itself, shifts, vanishes, and its almost spatial reality is made manifest in the pocket of mist cast far in the distance. I do not know if the boundaries of the hothouse are to be found on the skin or on the horizon, but the dusk-coloured flowers it cultivates behind its glass know nothing of the limits separating flesh from blood, love from the idea of love, an eyelid from a star – a ghostly flower that the beloved woman fixes to her spectral bosom without the internal movement this erotic act would presume losing its almost physical form. Shadows of oneiric images, a flower, genitals, a diamond, are transported on a wave I shall designate D because it belongs to Desire, Despair, and the Demon, the receiving and receptive factors being the horizontal lovers with their hair in a trance. What I call "wave" is perhaps in reality only an instantaneous leprosy, a simultaneous rat, and if scientists at the turn of the century defined the externalising of sensibility as a peculiar form of internalising, we should not forget that in the absence of new evidence, the letter D, like the word sensibility, remains a pure hypothesis. Because all letters and all words can be considered false hypotheses so long as objects are contradicted by impulses, so long as objects and images are not reserved for the sole use of the poet, the scientist, and the dreamer. The glowing reality of an object that has gone through a hospice window, when the madman on his iron bed shows his burns to a doctor who, with a knowing smile, is considering prescribing hydrotherapy! Even though they are visible and tangible, the doctor, his knowing smile, and the hydrotherapy are for me three false hypotheses that shall be swiftly rejected when the reality of an object – momentarily written in invisible ink on the black paper of the unknown – will no longer be in doubt.

Invisible flower, visible only through the deep-sea diver's eyelids that are thinner than water, I carry you far away at the speed of fever, to where my beloved, scarabs filling her eyes, her nostrils emitting two enormous leeches, sucks in your sharp scents, your cruel cantharidal sap.

At last the infantile game of daisy petals has lost its ambiguous nature, the choice between "she loves me" and "she loves me not" which strangled children in the fields, which raised doubt and dread to the level of a *Weltanschauung*, which tried to teach us an early lesson in fearing tomorrow, disillusionments, proverbs and all the moralising and sceptical forms that fell from the children's primers like tombstones, at last the infantile game of daisy petals is a certainty, its alternatives having been sorted to

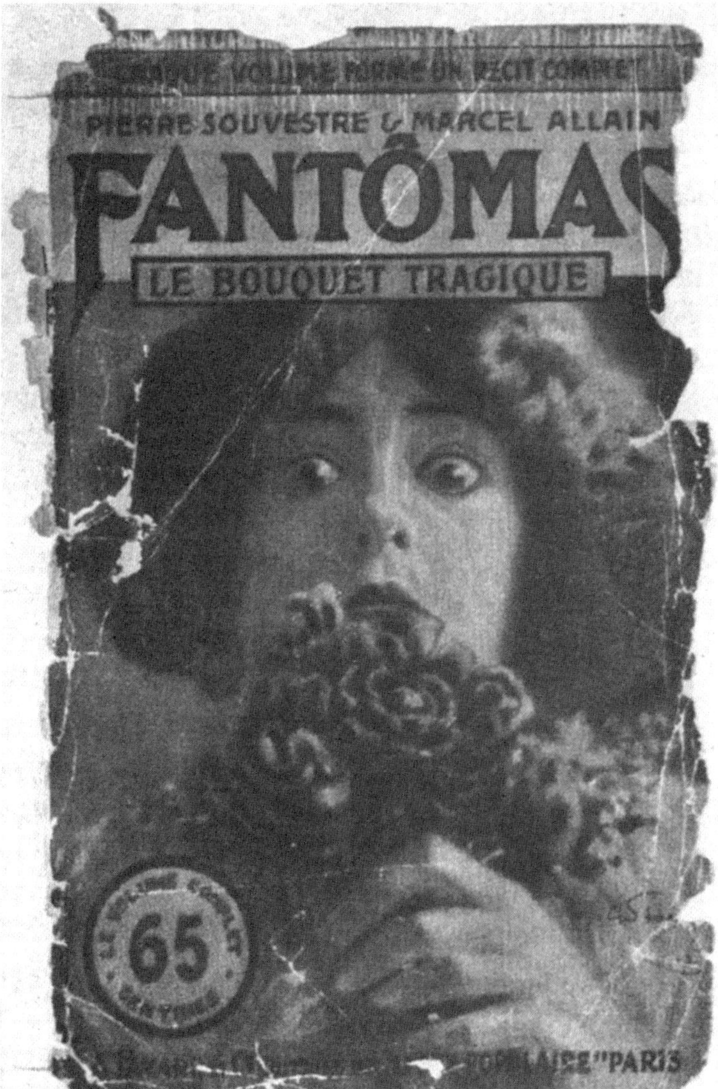

Fig. 15 The Tragic Bouquet

recombine in a way more thrilling than ever (gorging on each other and coupling): "you love me or you love me" – you love me or you love me, girl with two plaits climbing up to find the comb, with two breasts that meet my lips, with two nostrils out of which glides the same butterfly, with two ears into which penetrates the same voice, the same echo, with two thighs going up to the same sex; she loves me or she loves me is the sole choice I am able to accept, the sole choice so long as there is a refusal to consider the world a laboratory for sadistic experiments devised by an evil god, so long as they choose to consider the world an untamed forest of love – and I mean the word "forest" in every sense it suggests: metaphoric, symbolic, real, and virtual – an untamed forest of love with its affirmative daisies, daisies on the breasts, the trees, the dreams, with "I love you or I love you" written in letters of green rings on every petal.

"I wish to give Mme A. some flowers. Twice I felt myself give way: the first time by a cold shiver on the nape of my neck, the second by the familiar feeling you get when you suddenly stretch your legs or wake up. I concentrate again and I fall into a deep sleep." (Notes of an externalising subject.)

"At a quarter to midnight, moderate vibrations . . . I had the impression that the whitish cloud was trying to arrange itself better and I tried to assist it with my thoughts. A vision, in the space of a few seconds, of very bright lilac flowers. Emerging from the cloud was a hand, clenched as if with effort. Then an open hand, almost as material as a hand of flesh and blood. But the effort didn't last; you had to grab the picture as quick as a flash." (Notes of a receptive subject.)

Phantom flowers, these embalmed incubi and succubi, surprise us at night on a bed of soil like young fiancées raped just in time. Every nuptial chamber is a hothouse with its glass steamed over by a lover breathing from afar. The nostrils flare, the pollen comes. The breasts of the beloved rove around, the words of love recall the oceans' trees, men heave heavy but seemingly useless packing trunks. But to have nothing but eyes is useless in a universe where the moon is black, and claims of separating the perceptible from the imperceptible no longer take into account the secret mechanism of the retina. We must give our wandering gaze something of the impenetrable obscurity of the retina so that the eye no longer resembles a useless canker under the brow. Let's go hunting with a jet-black eye in the middle of our brow, and let it be seduced by images as if by snakes.

The woman's breasts rove, the man's eyes rove, and

their encounter produces a brief spark in the night. I light my cigarette with this hermaphroditic spark and run across my lips a young horse with testes longer than its mane. From between its hindquarters, a little giddy from the obstacle, slips the erotic horse with its flanks of corn. On its back it carries so many trunks that with each movement one comes undone and falls onto the street with open lid. The trunks appear empty, but at the very bottom the darkness is so palpable that it can be grasped, touched, weighed, felt. It measures 2.4 metres across. It has a fever. It has a scar on its shoulder. The darkness can be drunk from the trunk even though it is easier to drink it from a glass. It often goes "bang!" just to scare you. At other times there's an orgy. Teeth are no longer white in the dark. Birds of prey see trees turned upside down. Every eye has dark rings around it. Even fried eggs. You can lure an owl with a fork. It is night-time all day.

From these days that are nights, from these garret windows that are underground cellars and corridors, from these castles with their curtains permanently drawn across the windows and doors, where the darkness within is more solid than a lamp, rises up the terrifying and demented ear of Van Gogh. With what yellow hue have they been coloured, what blood has passed through them in its flow, in which flames have they bathed, in what swamps have they drowned, what ravenous insects, what subtle poisons have torn the woman's fingers at the very moment when between two obliterated objects she found the still burning ear of this delirious lover? At what hour might this have happened, how many crimes were committed at that instant, how many love letters were travelling the world at the moment when such a woman received this supreme homage?

For the first time, panicking humanity asked itself a question that sounded like a slip of the tongue: What is an ear? Is it a seashell? A trap? A buckle? An echo? Anatomy lays aside its unused instruments and seeks an equivalent in the shadows it projects within and onto people like a living mask. Can this organ stuck to people's heads be raised like a hat? Even if the auricle, Eustachian tube, and cochlea are as bizarre and as removed from us as the mammoth and the brontosaurus, are they not also just as ambiguous as the brim, the cap, and the ribbon? If one tried to decipher the subtle cryptogram posed by this part of the human body, in its baffling and provocative form, does not Van Gogh's gesture offer us the solution to the first part of the problem? If we assign the auricle as A, the Eustachian tube as E, the

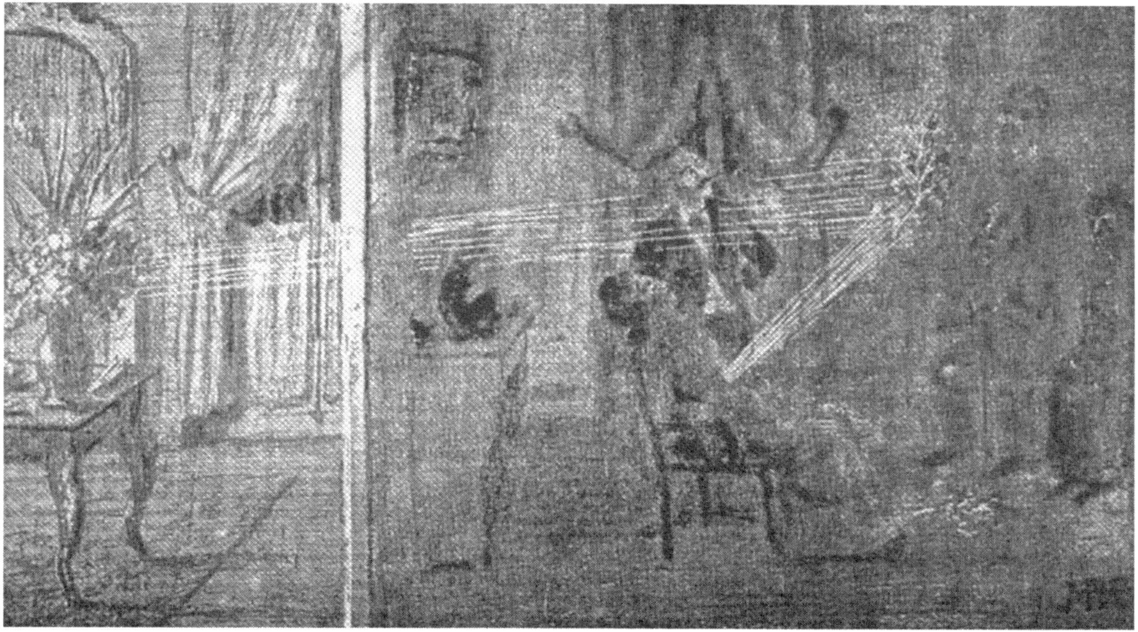

Fig. 16 Mechanism for the Bestowal of Flowers

cochlea as C and Van Gogh as G, all of this put into a formula gives us:

$$A = G/n - (E + C)$$

n being the number of organs. Designating the male sex organ as S^1 and the female as S^2, we have:

$$S = S_1 = -S^2$$

Three equivalent unknown quantities can be introduced into the equation:

$$S = S_1 = -S^2 = X$$

From this cryptogram posed by the human ear in general and that of Van Gogh's in particular, X is the first quantity that can lead us to the solution of the whole problem. I like badly-typed texts criss-crossed by rows of xxxxxxx because they give me the vague feeling of being confronted by a mystery. On the left-hand side of his head Van Gogh had a scar in the shape of an X. A woman receives an X of blood from him. His tortured landscapes are immense plantations of Xs. Kisses from the beloved in the form of an X. Poems written solely with the letter X. All dreams belong in the category X. A perfect crime is a calligraphic X. The existence of X justifies our own. Without X the world would be forever condemned to retain the demoralising nature of current society.

I come closer to get a better look at this fascinating X just below the painter's temple. I see a transparent ear, made of fog or smoke, from which hangs an earring encrusted with rubies. In the middle of the earring is a winking eye, each wink producing a little ripple on the waters of the precious stones from which there then falls a drop of blood, giving the ensemble the look of a sieve through which filters the auburn hair of a woman. The whole arrangement is covered by a fairly large glass bowl that could contain fish of various colours and species, and accompanied by a telescope through which one could see inside each fish. A certain number of lenses attached to the telescope give the illusion that the interior of each fish is populated with plants, insects, or stones, depending on the lens' optical angle. I saw a fish whose insides had been gnawed away by a spider and I understood what leprosy meant. I saw plant sprigs that were too much for the animal to contain growing out through the fish scales. The glass bowl, the screen for this landscape in which cruelty is a slow, geological art, is covered by a parasol, probably a strange plant or a sleeping animal.

This chaotic imprint of the offered ear now resembles an overturned horse sniffed by a cat. The echo of the ear resonates below Van Gogh's temple like the death rattle of dry swamps. Love finds a way through these mutilating symbols and stumbles out of this adventure stupefied. The plants, animals, and trains of every speed pass through each other without colliding. Love rubs up against the steel of the carriages, against the nettles and the fur. Its mutilated and mutilating aspects are well known to those lovers with flagellated blood cells, with their fingernails torn. If I were to reconstitute Van Gogh's ear,* this terrifying object offered to a lover, this sublime homage of the flagellated lovers, I would choose a substance that would not lack either ruby, nettle, or smoke. At the same time, I would like to make two ears out of excrement for Beethoven and, also with excrement, an ear mounted on a plinth that might symbolise – perhaps too explicitly but not enough to be insulting – that cretinising preoccupation that goes by the name of music.

* The artistic myth of Van Gogh the *painter* is of no concern to me.

Only a few months have passed since the monstrous roads I travel led my wavering steps towards this atrocious and dreadful person, this apparition of shadow and ferocity who would become my sole travelling companion, my sole aspiration, for the rest of my life. With my head bent over my signature in blood, every night I would call up the face of this dark lover; my drowned man's lips would often kiss the traces of his cape of flames, a seal marking my pact. Little did I know then the mystery of this sudden abandonment, and in my solitude Satan was the mirror in which I sought myself before falling asleep; Satan was the dream I could still recall the following day. I knew this game was an outmoded trap sprung by the ideas of good and evil to test us; I knew at the last minute the Devil would resume his customary relations with me. During the night of November 2, in the classic guise of a messenger, there appeared an extremely beautiful woman, her beauty unreal, mad and lucid, one of those women the popular imagination has inevitably identified with infernal forces, the kind of woman whose approach suddenly flings me into the most nebulous regions of my being, the place where desire is simultaneously ash and flame, at whose approach I forget everything I once knew, since everything was to be rediscovered and reinvented. Nothing was familiar to me any

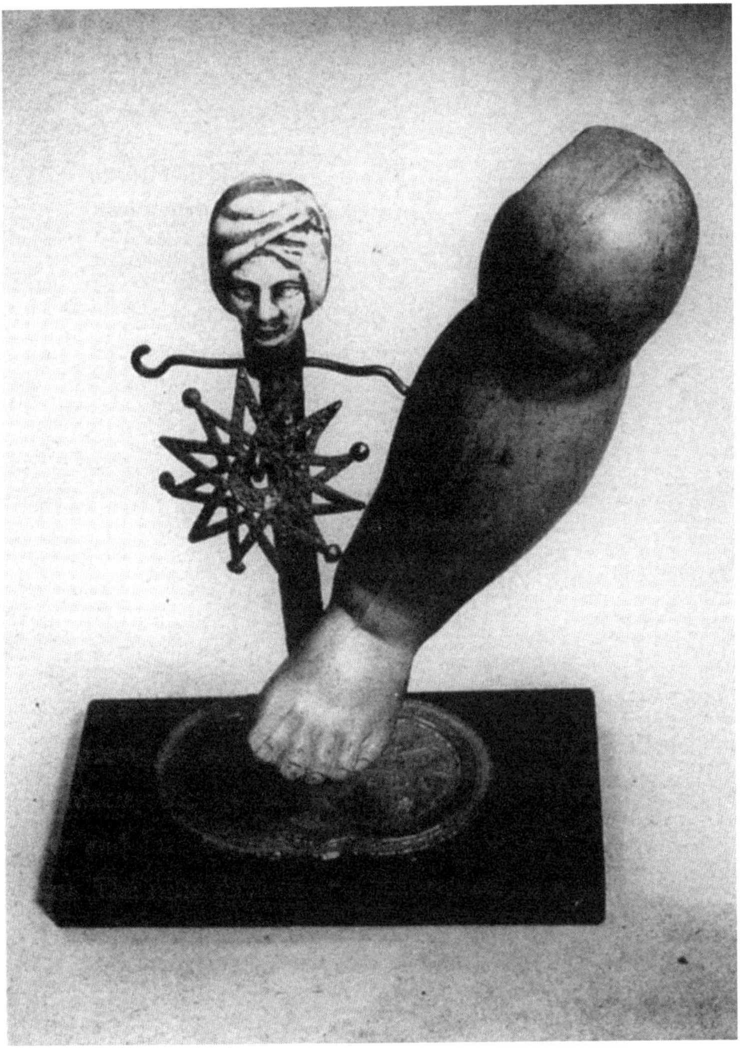

Fig. 17 Déline-Fetish

longer, nothing was repeated, not a single fact was put to me or a single premise; we are buffeted in a universe bereft of reference points, forms, or solid bodies, where even among the most basic ideas and elements nothing has yet emerged from the chaos, all is completely unknown, all is completely obscure. In the instant I met Déline, I learned that mystery is a woman, since the first door I opened and closed in the shadows was, in a way that was not at all symbolic, our first night of love.[21]

One Sunday afternoon I was invited to a female friend's house and I decided to accept, particularly when I was assured that D. would be there, a striking woman who had long attracted me. I would have gone anyway, since those afternoons when one might drink and meet women tempt me in that they are pleasantly mind numbing, tedious as a phonograph record.

But at 4 o'clock that Sunday I did not go to her house. I preferred to visit different friends in whose company I felt comfortable. My friend would be annoyed, but I would explain that it made no sense to come simply because I had promised to. Around 10 that evening I suddenly got to my feet. I insisted to my wife that she accompany me. She agreed unwillingly, claiming to feel sleepy and exhausted. At last we went out into the dark, rainy, late autumn weather. We arrived at our friend's house soaking wet, and there we met a few women and men gathered in an atmosphere of vague intoxication. D. had left half an hour before with D., the man who had brought Déline. Déline. I sit beside Déline, I stroke Déline, I kiss Déline, I leave with Déline, I make love to Déline. There are no obstacles, no mutilating people or objects, no aspects of the catastrophe the external world might adopt in intimate relations between a man and a woman. Truly detached from anything external that might contradict an individual, our daily encounters took place in that infantile sphere where lovers agree to meet and where the erotic act signals the end and a new beginning of the game. For me the few hours separating us between encounters were an unbearable torment because at their end waited Déline, as fresh and agile, as mad and lucid as a crystal. I could only feed myself when she was beside me, and from the moment I was apart from her I was seized with a fit of nervous yawning that belied my insomnia. There were always rare, choice dishes and drinks beside her bed, all the more surprising in a house where usually very little was eaten.

Conversation was generally superficial and, when it came to a discussion of what one might call more fundamental matters, we were surprised at the unexpected mutual understanding of two people whose anxieties bordered on the manic. This young woman of 21 had the experience in love of a 40-year-old and the mind of an initiate. It was pleasant to watch this agile body in slumber. It was pleasant to see nightfall on her lightly singed hair. I adored everything she said, everything she did, and I believe this total admiration for Déline was not simply the result of the customary overvaluation of one's erotic object. I believed Déline to be truly wonderful. I loved Déline and could not comprehend everyone else's passive immobility, that of my friends least of all; without meaning to, I now classified them as belonging to that stage of general paralysis afflicting the rest of humanity. I failed to understand how one could gaze calmly at objects, fingers, or shadows while my eyes darted down and back up to my eyelids with the speed of a bullet. I failed to understand why people were not yet dead, why people had not yet been invented. I am aroused by practically all men, Déline told me, and all of a sudden this human clay bound up in trousers and pathetic concerns grew before my eyes as though seen through a magnifying glass. Coming close to this woman with her mathematically precise instincts gave these men their identities. I lit her a cigarette. We went to a cinema showing *Fantômas.* I tore at her stockings, I ruffled her hair. I forgot to avert my gaze from her eyes and I couldn't tell who was the hypnotiser and who the hypnotised. I saw (in my first waking dream) Déline execute the steps of a tam-tam dance in a room of indeterminate colour. She was totally naked, her hair dishevelled. On the walls were crystal vases filled with eggs into which she thrust her hands. She pulled out one after another and smashed them one at a time on top of her head. She was surrounded in juices and faint smells. I saw (in my second waking dream) Déline dressed in a fish tank full of goldfish. Only her arms and legs peeped out of the tank, clad in a tight black body stocking. The walls of the room in which she was moving were covered with clocks of various sizes, their dials reversed as if in a mirror. On a pedestal on the left, a naked man sat bolt upright in a chair. Next to him was an old man with long white hair dressed as a Renaissance Italian aristocrat. His beard was knotted around the first man's immobilised hands. At the seated man's feet was a child in swaddling bands, signs of recent strangulation evident on its throat. Déline moved around this torture chamber with slow, unreal gestures. Defying the laws of gravity, her steps were as if projected in slow motion. Slowly, very slowly, she leant her body slightly forward, and the water and the fish started to spill from the tank. Like a long-awaited magic sign and as though it were

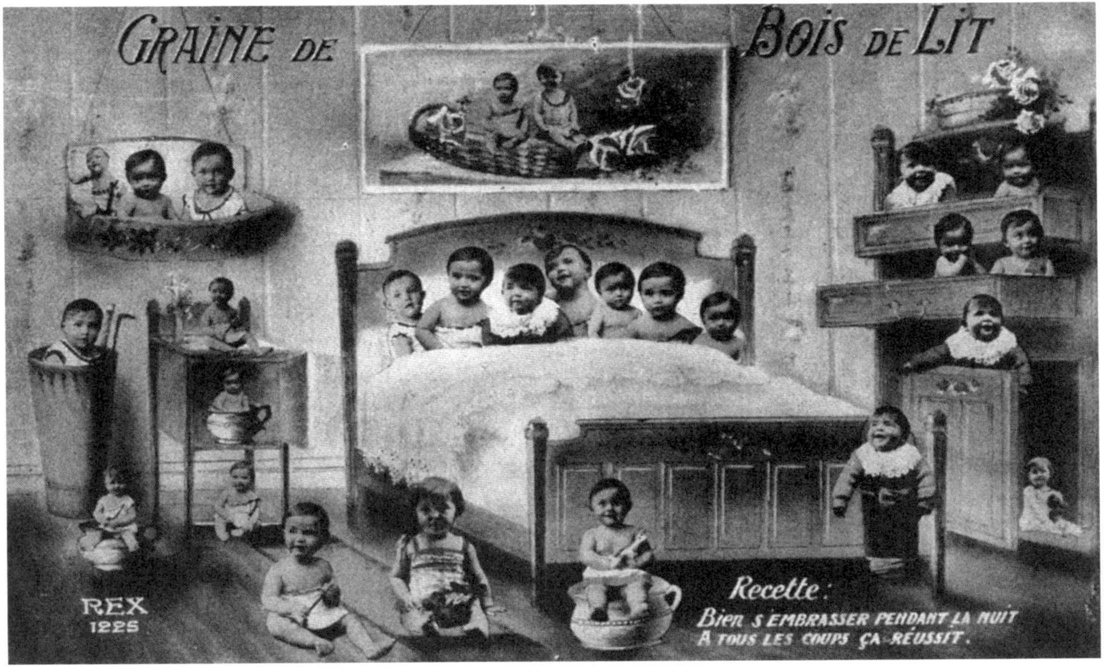

Fig. 18 Déline's Reply

all part of the same obscure mechanism, the pedestal with its three people on it started to rise up. The dance finished when the last drop had been poured from the fish tank and, while the trio had gone through the ceiling, Déline disappeared with the same slow, unreal movements into one of the numerous clocks on the wall.

I kiss Déline and I forget to withdraw my lips. I make love to Déline and I forget to finish. I don't want to finish anything. A world with no beginning, in which every gesture has the infinite duration of the impossible and every breath is hard as a diamond, must never end. I bring her an object entitled Déline-Fetish (fig. 17). In exchange she gives me a postcard depicting 27 children (fig. 18). An hour later it was all over. I could not understand why we had to part, when in fact neither of us wanted this rupture to happen, when no-one we knew objected to our affair. After nine days of love I was left alone, unable to understand what had happened or what would happen next, tormented by the unfathomable mystery looming all around me like a forest, and I fell into an interpretative delirium lasting two days and nights, at the end of which humanity's ignorance was revealed to me under its supremely demoralising guise – the darkness surrounding us proved to be as terrifying and as heavy as an empty balloon.

Like a distant echo I could sense that the events I had participated in over these last few days went far beyond what one had hitherto understood by the concept of love. I could not tell which part of it was love and which part magic; I could not discern either the place where these two dreadful variations of black joined or where they separated, but I am certain that each lover must also be a magician in order to approach fearlessly these sublime metamorphoses of shadow. What were the contradictory forces that had appeared on that unremarkable afternoon, what phenomenon with its almost chemical precision was burning within me with no regard for my person? What mystery of chance was trying to reveal itself? What set of desires had appeared just then, like a pack of wolves, in the universe? What secret was alchemically emerging to brush lightly against a profane being? Defying humanity, Satan, running his monogrammed glove through my hair, left me nothing but the superficial pleasure of things, and now I found myself alone again with nothing but the rustle of questions and their inverted images.

I did not go to my friend's house that Sunday afternoon, even though I wanted to, and even though all of my expressed desires should have led me to. I only went at 10 o'clock that evening because, in the meantime, the woman

D., who was my reason for going, had left with D., the man who had arrived with Déline. All of the obstacles that might have prevented or delayed our meeting were to vanish on their own. This obscure mechanism, one that the Angels of the Shadows refuse to reveal to me, operated slowly but surely, setting up every coincidence. It brought together those hands that had to touch, it drew aside the people and objects that might have startled those hands and scared them away. But all the same, I do not know why I knew Déline, and the perfection of this machinery of chance terrifies me. One year earlier I had found a magician's head from which I was to make an object intended for my friend Hérold.[22] I knew the object had to be made for Hérold, but I did not know how to make it. The magician's head remained in its drawer until that moment. Once I got it out, I immediately found the elements it needed so I could give it to Déline. Through the intervention of the object I learned that the desire to know Déline had been present in me even before I knew of her existence in the world. The object was only apparently destined for Hérold. The set of unknown quantities, the desire to know Déline among them, was only using Hérold's name for the purpose of revealing to me the object's true destination: Déline Hérault (Hérold, Hérault). It was a set of unknown quantities in which the desire was only partially present, because the phenomena attached to this object seemed so obscure and frightening to me that it was impossible not to suspect magic. What I have in mind is a magic that is perhaps not unconnected with the libido; but for as long as the forces in play kept their ashen mask I could only speak about them in obscurantist terms. I have always had the sensation of being thought like Lautréamont* and Rimbaud,** but it had never happened to me before that this other who thought me should leave my being and appear in front of me in a concrete and tangible way like any other external object. This time it was *Déline-Fetish* that thought me. It determined and took decisions that were beyond me, that dumbfounded me. Perhaps this fetish's magical property drew its tangled roots from the depths of my being, but so long as its strength outstripped the abilities of my psychic mechanisms, seemingly setting itself in opposition to the latter, my affective relationship towards it was plainly fetishistic, equivalent to the obscurantism of primitive man worshipping his own dread.

I was afraid and could not understand this magic object that had separated me from Déline. Without my knowledge, this magic object was gradually becoming an agent of sorcery

* "People think me."[23]
** "I is someone else."

and, along the same vague and obscure lines of force, the object given to me by Déline had transformed itself into an agent of counter-sorcery, reversing all of the expectations of love and mortally wounding the lover-magician. In psychic terms, neither of us could understand the rupture between us, which was ungrounded and unwanted, but this ill-fated meeting of objects commanded and arranged everything, using both of us like two automata merely executing somnambulistic movements which were no doubt necessary but entirely contrary. In the light of these vague revelations, the object offered by Déline was trying to tell me something, but all my efforts to discern a figure in these whispers failed. Déline had given me a postcard showing 27 children (no doubt representing the genitals of her past lovers), a card she had found by chance that afternoon at the home of an acquaintance. All alone in the room for a moment, I casually turned the card over, expecting to find some banal text. The message was a few years old, and was an invitation to Paris; to my total stupefaction, it was signed "Hérold." The same fundamental formula had been used to concoct both poisons.

I knew that I could grasp only the outlines of this formula and that the mutations produced within it remained secret to me. I knew that the phenomenon's external aspect was its only quality that could gladden my heart and that the combustions taking place deep within it would continue unseen by me and without my knowing consent. The ill-fated exchange of objects destroyed itself, and in feeling its mortal effects I was on the point of tears, of despair; the lovers drank the poison draft without death ever requiring that they possess detailed pharmaceutical knowledge of it. I was blundering around in a tangle of events that escaped me; I was inhaling herbs the shape of whose roots I did not know; I was taking part in a ritual with massive magical import but whose contents remained beyond my grasp. My gestures may have been those of an initiate; I carried out the slightest details as though I understood why, but only I knew how terrified I was of the precipice between the determinant and the determined, and how strange, mysterious, and dark my own movements seemed to me. So what sacred game was I taking part in every evening when choice dishes and rare and exquisite beverages were being brought to the nuptial bed? It is not possible to speak of coincidence when I know that meals in that house usually consisted of nothing but tea. But for whom was this real or symbolic sacrifice being made? Who did we fear, from which gods were we seeking benevolent favours, which evil spirits were threatening us – and was this the legion of lovers, each abandoned in their turn with the most recent lover at their head, threatening as a gaping wound, like a half-murdered father? And what of the sacred dances in my waking dreams, to which primitive necessities did they correspond? What magic formula was being acted out? What secret was trying to pierce through this hallucinatory and hermetic language? The desire to despoil, the sadistic desire to fill the beloved woman with sperm, as psychoanalysis informs me, cannot fully account for the substance of these two sacred dances that are rooted profoundly in the jungle and the pyramids. I had the sensation of having unconsciously repeated a ritual an inhabitant of the jungle and the pyramids would have executed with precise intentions. Without knowing it, I had touched the same levers covered with spiders and living hieroglyphs, but the sounds they triggered off scared no-one but myself. My delirium of interpretation was the response of a man terrified of his own audacity, the attempt to attain the seeming calm of an initiate and bite mystery on the shoulder as if it were a woman. The nine days of love during which my freedom had exceeded even the hopes I placed in poetry and revolution, a limitless, total, infernal freedom, seem to me the mirror reverse of the nine days I had spent in prison nine years earlier because of love, because of my poems about love that my contemporaries had cited in their legal briefs as a case of the assault on common decency.[24] From this battle between the demon of freedom and the god of prison there emerged, as if to justify my delirium of interpretation, the obsessive number 9, designated by the calculations of the black Kabbalah as an entirely analytical number and, all-powerful beneath its crystal cape, with its comet's red eye, there also emerged LOVE, mad and lucid, real and virtual, living and dead like Déline's hair. As Déline, the indecipherable ghost of love, fell asleep on my shoulder she darkened the darkness.

November 18, 1941

TRANSLATOR'S NOTES

Introduction

1 There does seem to be one exception to the claim that the *The Passive Vampire* is an entirely faithful account, and it is a significant one. It would appear that the woman named here as Déline, the presiding enchantress of the book's conclusion, did not in fact bear that name; see note 21 below.

2 I have written more extensively on this subject in "From Sorcery to Silence: The Objects of Gherasim Luca," *Modern Language Review*, vol. 88, 3 (July 1993): 625-38.

3 Letter to Jacques Hérold, Bucharest 22 February 1940, cited in the sale catalogue *Collection Jacques Hérold*, Paris Druout Richelieu, November 13, 1998, lot 186.

4 The reader will doubtless note the significant fact that several of the objects, and a recipient of two of them, A. (Luca's wife Antonia perhaps?) are not discussed in the text, and that there is no figure 10.

The Passive Vampire

1 Luca is clearly referring here to the categories of "surrealist objects" enumerated by the French Surrealist Group, in particular those described by André Breton, Salvador Dalí, and Alberto Giacometti in the issue of *Le Surréalisme au service de la Révolution* (no. 4, December 1931) that first highlighted the question of the object.

2 Comte de Lautréamont, *Poésies,* translated by Alexis Lykiard (London: Allison & Busby, 1978), 75.

3 Objective chance is the key surrealist principle by which apparently coincidental events both reveal the patterns of desire and guide its fulfillment in the everyday world – in André Breton's definition "the form making manifest the exterior necessity which traces its path in the human unconscious," in *Mad Love,* translated by Mary Ann Caws (Lincoln: University of Nebraska Press, 1987), 23.

4 V. is the painter Victor Brauner (1903-1966), a member of the Parisian surrealist group during the 1930s and the most important link between surrealism in Paris and Bucharest. Brauner's brother, Théodore, was the photographer for *The Passive Vampire*'s illustrations. This and the following identifications have been made with the invaluable help of Antonia Rasicovici.

5 Hélène is Elena, the wife of the poet Virgil Teodorescu of the Bucharest surrealist group, and a close friend of the Lucas.

6 P. is the poet and artist Paul Paun (1915–1994), a member of the Romanian Surrealist Group.

7 G. is the poet Gellu Naum (1915–2001), founding member with Luca of the Romanian Surrealist Group, and who, like Luca, had lived in Paris between 1938–39.

8 C.N. is the poet Constantin Nisipeanu (1907–1998), connected with the avant-garde Unu group in the late twenties and early thirties, to which the younger writers of Luca's generation had also been drawn.

9 A.B. is the poet Aureliu Baranga (1913–1979), a friend of Luca from the time of the Alge group in the early 1930s.

10 André Breton, *Nadja,* translated by Richard Howard (London: Penguin, 1999), 105-6 and 109. The passage in question relates to one of Nadja's mediumistic drawings, and one is also drawn to the information on adjoining pages that Nadja, originally from Lille, first met Breton on the rue Lafayette, and tells him soon afterwards of how an admirer used to call her Lena.

11 *L'anatomie de la lettre* does not seem to figure in any of Luca's bibliographies, so one might presume that like several other projects this book was at least partially written but never published.

12 There is a clear allusion here to the "symbolically functioning objects" first proposed by Salvador Dalí. See *Le Surréalisme au service de la Révolution,* 4 (December 1931): 16-17.

13 The earthquake of November 10, 1940 measured 7.4 on the Richter scale and caused severe damage to the whole of Bucharest.

14 Sigmund Freud, *The Interpretation of Dreams* (Harmondsworth: Penguin, 1976), 529. Part of this passage had also been cited by André Breton in *Les Vases communicants* (1932) in connection with the interpretation of dream objects.

15 One of the earliest of many games played by surrealists, "exquisite corpse" is a variation of "consequences" in which players either write a phrase or draw a section of a body on a sheet of paper before hiding the results from the next player to create a composite sentence or image.

16 A reference to the famous quote from Lautréamont and a watchword for surrealist practice, "As beautiful . . . as the chance meeting on a dissecting-table of a sewing-machine and an umbrella," *Maldoror,* translated by Alexis Lykiard (London: Allison and Busby, 1970), 177 (slightly modified here).

17 Marquis de Sade, *Justine,* translated by Richard Seaver and Austryn Wainhouse (New York: Grove Press, 1965), 516.

18 Fantômas, legendary creation of thriller novelists Marcel Allain and Pierre Souvestre in a series of books (and later films) from 1911 onwards, was a perennial favourite of the surrealists for the ruthless poetry of his criminal genius.

19 This and the following quotation, though apparently not the third,

come from Chapter 19 of J.-K. Huysmans, *Là-Bas* (*The Damned,* 1891). [Translations my own.]

20 Gilles de Rais was the infamous fifteenth-century French nobleman and soldier executed in 1440 for the mass torture and murder of large numbers of children; Rose Keller was the young widow propositioned, abducted and attacked by the Marquis de Sade, Easter 1768, a crime for which he was charged and imprisoned; Des Esseintes is the disaffected anti-hero of J.-K. Huysmans' symbolist novel *À Rebours* (*Against Nature,* 1884).

21 Déline was most likely Nadine Krainik, a young woman also connected with Paul Paun. According to Antonia Rasicovici, she was an outsider to the Romanian Surrealist Group, and considered by some members as an unwelcome intruder (though she was subse-quently a participant in the postwar Parisian group, signing several important collective tracts in 1947 and 1948). While it is reasonable to suppose that Luca changed her name here to protect those involved, one might note the echo between Déline's real name and that of Nadja. Of partially French origin – which is presumably why Luca later ascribes her a French surname – Krainik apparently helped bring Luca's possessions to Paris after his move there in the early 1950s. See also Petre Raileanu, *Gherasim Luca* (Paris: Oxus 2004), 97, note 71.

22 The painter Jacques Hérold (1910-1987) had participated in the Bucharest Unu group at the end of the 1920s before leaving for Paris where he would eventually join the French surrealists. Like Brauner, Hérold would become one of Luca's closest comrades after his own permanent move to Paris.

23 Not, in fact, Lautréamont but Arthur Rimbaud, from a letter to Georges Izambard, May 13, 1871, in *Complete Works, Selected Letters,* translated by Wallace Fowlie (Chicago: University of Chicago Press, 1966), 303. The following quote is from the same letter, p. 305.

24 The public scandal of the summer of 1933 that resulted when Luca and his friends from the pre-surrealist Alge group sent copies of their texts to notable personalities – including a former Prime Minister – cost them a brief prison sentence but without, it would seem, incurring serious consequences. See Raileanu, *Gherasim Luca,* 69-71.

ABOUT THE AUTHOR

Ghérasim Luca was born July 23, 1913 in Bucharest into a liberal Jewish family. Fluent in Yiddish, Romanian, German, and French, he traveled frequently to Paris in the late 1930s where he became acquainted with the surrealists. World War II and Romania's official anti-Semitism forced Luca into internal exile. During the short pre-Communist period of Romanian independence, he joined Gellu Naum, Paul Paun, Virgil Teodorescu, and Dolfi Trost in founding the Romanian Surrealist Group, and in 1945, Luca and Trost co-authored the group's principal text, *Dialetics of the Dialectic.* Finally able to leave Romania in 1952, he moved to Paris via Israel. Having spent forty years in France without papers, he was evicted from his apartment in 1994, as were all the building's tenants, officially for "urban renewal." Now 80 and unable to cope with his new situation, Luca committed suicide on February 9, 1994 by jumping in the Seine.

ABOUT THE TRANSLATOR

Krzysztof Fijałkowski teaches at the Norwich University of the Arts. He has written extensively on the interwar avant-garde and is the co-editor of *Surrealism against the Current: Tracts and Declarations.* His translations include Michel Surya's *Georges Bataille: An Intellectual Biography* and *Refusal of the Shadow: Surrealism and the Caribbean* (both with Michael Richardson).

THE PASSIVE VAMPIRE

Ghérasim Luca

Translated and introduced by Krzysztof Fijałkowski

Originally published in French as *Le Vampire passif*
by Éditions de l'Oubli, Bucharest, 1945

Cover and design by Jed Slast
Set in Garamond BE

SECOND PRINTING, 2022

First published in 2008 by
TWISTED SPOON PRESS
P.O. Box 21 – Preslova 12
15000 Prague 5, Czech Republic
www.twistedspoon.com

IMAGE TO WORD 1

Printed and bound in the Czech Republic
by Protisk

Distributed to the trade by
CENTRAL BOOKS
www.centralbooks.com

SCB DISTRIBUTORS
www.scbdistributors.com

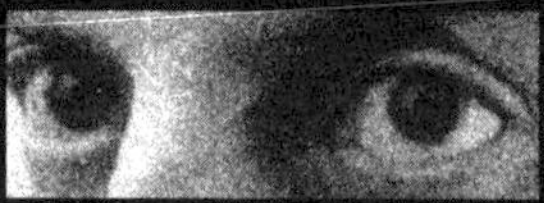